I0625958

The Orchard's Secret

Templa Melnick

BROKEN YOKE

PUBLISHING

The Orchard's Secret

Copyright © 2021 by Templa Melnick
All rights reserved.

Published by Broken Yoke Publishing, LLC.
BrokenYokePublishing.com

This publication is the intellectual property of the author. No part of this publication may be resold, reproduced in any form, stored in a retrieval system, or transmitted by any means, without the prior written permission of the author. Doing such would constitute theft and is illegal.

This is a work of fiction. All characters and incidents are the product of the author's imagination and any resemblance to actual events, people (living or dead), is entirely coincidental. The author's use of real locales and reference to existing entities is done with the greatest respect.

ISBN: 978-1-955941-00-6

Dedication

To Hunter, Tucker, Brooke, Avery and Grace. You fill my world with love and laughter.

Acknowledgements

I owe an enormous debt of gratitude to my husband, Chris, for not letting me give up on this story – even though it took years to find its way onto the page. And to my wildly supportive and understanding family, thank you. Thank you for eating peanut butter sandwiches when I was so absorbed in my imaginary world that I forgot to fix dinner. Thank you for *all* of the sacrifices you've made so that I can chase this crazy dream.

My deepest and most heartfelt thanks to my kind and wise Word Weavers tribe: Darlia Sawyer, Debra Lueck, Jessica Bertrand, Sandy DuBois, Joe Bowden, Stephanie Floyd, Andy DeWitt, Susan Carter, Lee Ann Womack. Your insights, corrections and willingness to plow through my rough drafts are priceless gifts. I'm not only a better writer because of you, but a better person. This world is a more beautiful place – and filled with riveting and grammatically-correct stories – because of each of you.

My village of eagle-eyed early readers, (especially Max and Kate!) deserve medals of honor. Thank you! Your suggestions, insights, and error-catching propelled this book to a higher level of excellence.

I wouldn't let anyone read this story before my long-suffering editor and dear friend, Denise Payne, had smoothed the rough edges. Thanks Denise, for trudging through my first drafts with such kindness and grace. You are a wise and wonderful friend.

I'd like to thank Shana, from Mesa County Sheriff's Department, for responding to my random questions at all hours. (I'd like to mention that all errors or deviations from actual law enforcement procedure in this book are mine, and mine alone. Don't blame Shana!)

And a very special thank you to my for-a-lifetime friend, Jennifer, for allowing me to use her family's names for the characters in this story. Even though time and distance have kept us apart physically, the bond we share as sisters-in-the-Lord remains as strong as ever. What a rare and precious treasure, indeed.

Chapter 1

I'm regretting drinking that Gatorade before we left. I mean, *really* wishing I hadn't. We're in the middle of the nothingness that separates Delta from Grand Junction. The mountains of Lake City, Colorado are disappearing behind us as we barrel down the highway towards my aunt's house in Palisade.

My older brother, Alex, is driving. Mom thinks it's a good opportunity for him to get some highway driving. Having a teen-aged driver behind the wheel for the past two hours is not helping my bladder situation. *At all.*

I rub the just-shaved stubble on the sides of my head. I like the way my hair bristles across my fingertips and try to let the victory of the buzz-cut distract me from the pressure in my bladder that makes me wiggle in my seat. I think I won the hair-cut battle when I told Mom to consider how much money she would save in hair gel. It takes a lot of hair gel to slick down that ridiculous cowlick of mine. And with middle school just a couple of months away, I need to find my own look. Not that I care much what I look like, but still.

At this moment, I wish I could be like Trey. My little brother is slumped in the corner of the Jeep with his face pressed against the seatbelt. Snoring. It's like a superpower with him. Ten minutes into any road trip, and he's asleep. He won't wake up until we get to Aunt Bekki's house. Even when I was his age, I don't think I could sleep like that.

The view whizzing past my window is barren, rocky fields with a few cows scattered here and there. No rest areas, no gas stations, no convenience stores anywhere in sight. And even though we stopped in Montrose just a half hour ago, I need another bathroom break.

"Mom, I need to stop."

The rearview mirror gives me a close up of her brown eyes as she rolls them and sighs. "There's no place to stop, Brandon. We'll be there in about forty minutes."

"I can't wait that long."

We lock eyes in the mirror, and she must see my desperation. "Alex, pull over to the side of the road. There's a spot up ahead. Make sure to signal."

"There's not another car in sight!"

"Use the turn signal anyway." Mom's voice has the don't-argue tone. "You never know when a car is going to pop over the hill."

I hear the click-click-click of the turn signal. Alex glares at me as he checks over his shoulder and then eases the Jeep to the side of the road. As soon as the Jeep slows, I pop off my seatbelt. The moment the tires stop moving, I bolt out the door to the nearest clump of bushes. *No more Gatorade before car trips for me.*

I'm surprised that Mom is behind the wheel of the Jeep when I get back in. Alex is riding shotgun, and he doesn't look happy about it. With a sigh of relief, I buckle my seatbelt. The last forty minutes of the trip should be easier. I'm definitely more comfortable now, and with Mom behind the wheel, I can finally relax.

Mom pulls onto the highway and says "Call Bek." The car obediently dials the number and Aunt Bekki's cheerful voice echoes through the small space as she picks up.

"Hello, Jen! Where are you guys?"

"Hey, Bek. We're in between Delta and Grand Junction, and you know how spotty cell coverage is through here. If I lose you, try me back in a minute. I just wanted to let you know we're running a bit behind schedule." Mom winks at me in the rear-view mirror. "We've had to make a few extra stops."

"Oh." Static crackles through the speaker as Aunt Bek adds, "I have to be at the airport in a couple of hours. Why don't we just meet at Aunt Sarah's place? You can drop me at the airport from there. I'll arrange to have someone pick up my car."

"Okay. We'll meet at Aunt Sarah's. See you soon!" Mom pushes the button to disconnect the call. "Alex, could you plug this address into the navigation? I always miss the turn." She hands him her cell phone with Aunt Sarah's contact information and Alex fiddles with the buttons on the Jeep's navigation screen while Mom drives. "All of these letters and crazy fractions for road names confuse me. I mean, 35 8/10 Road, G 7/10 Road. You wouldn't think those were actual streets, but in Mesa County they are."

Opening my eyes what seems like a few minutes later, I realize we're off the highway and meandering through a peach orchard. The Jeep bumps across a dirt road and a huge house appears through the trees. Two towering pine trees on either side of the porch make me think of old soldiers standing guard over a fairy-tale castle, frowning as the Jeep kicks up a cloud of dust in the quiet, sleepy orchard. I roll my eyes at my over-active imagination. *Get a grip, Brandon.*

We pull into a circular gravel driveway behind Aunt Bekki's mud-splattered Chevy Traverse. My cousin Kyle races across the grass to meet us. He's all arms and legs, like one of those gazelles on a documentary about the African savanna. Kyle is four months younger than I am but he's definitely taller. Last time I saw him, I was the tall one. Thirteen is a weird age.

Kyle yanks the door of the Jeep open. "Finally! You're here!" His brown eyes are bright with excitement as he tugs on my arm. "This is gonna be so great! An entire month of the Cousin Crew. Trey! Wake up!"

Kyle stands on the running board and leans over me to grab Trey's arm. My nose crinkles as Kyle's breath fills the small space. *Did he even brush his teeth this morning?* I do a quick breath-check in my hand to make sure it's not me turning the interior of the Jeep into a gas chamber.

Trey stretches and yawns. I don't know how he can even move after being a human pretzel for the past three hours. I guess that's what it's like when you're still a little kid of ten.

Wiggling past Kyle, my red high-tops hit the gravel driveway. Inhaling a huge lungful of peach-scented air, I stretch my arms over my head. Aunt Bekki rushes in to give me a hug. She smells nice, like coconut shampoo. "Oh, my goodness. You're almost as tall as me."

That's not saying much. My aunt is only a couple of inches taller than Mom. But I smile anyway.

Before I can think of something to say to Aunt Bekki, Kyle yanks me onto the grass and slams me to the ground. *I should have seen that coming*. He laughs and tries to pin my arms. But muscle memory kicks in, and I flip him into a *Tate-shiho-gatame* hold that looks like an on-the-ground-hug if you're not familiar with Judo. Ha! Kyle might be bigger than me, but I'm the one with the green belt.

Trey jumps on top of me, and I throw him off with a wild roar. We punch and roll around on the ground until, panting to catch my breath, I hear Mom's voice.

"Who is *that*?"

Something about the tone of her voice catches my attention. Kyle and Trey must have noticed too, because we all stop wrestling to watch the gleaming black Suburban that pulls up behind our Jeep.

Standing, I brush off the dry grass that's stuck to my jeans. This is not your everyday Suburban. It's all black; the grill across the front, the wheels, and the luggage rack across the top.

"Wow. It looks kinda like the ones the President rides in." Trey's voice is barely above a whisper, but it seems loud in the silence that has fallen on the group. "Or the bad guys in the movies."

We can't pull our eyes away from the intimidating black vehicle, but we're now behind the front end of the Chevy. Like we know we need to put some distance – and a large metal object – between us and this vehicle.

A collective gasp goes out from our group when the front door opens. A man with dark, slicked-back hair and bulging muscles stands beside the SUV. His sunglasses glint in the afternoon light as he turns towards us.

Kyle grabs my arm and hisses in my ear, "He looks like Duane Johnson in that movie we saw." I nod. If Duane *the Rock* Johnson has a scary older brother, this could be him.

The driver's voice is deep and raspy. "My boss is here to speak to Sarah Hooper."

Kyle's fingers dig into my arm. He croaks out, "That's our aunt."

"Get her." The driver crosses his massive arms across his chest. "Now." I can't pull my eyes away from the snake tattoo that encircles his bicep. When his muscle moves, so does the snake. Creepy.

Kyle walks across the yard like his legs are heavy, and he stumbles on the porch steps because he's still gawking at the strange Suburban.

The rear window eases down, and suddenly I'm staring into the face of a man in the back seat. He has sharp cheekbones and a nose like a hawk's beak. His eyes glitter in the shadowy interior and as his dark, cold eyes meet mine, I shiver.

His heavily accented voice cuts through the stunned silence. "Move it, leetle boy! I am in a hurry." The man's voice ripples through the air and even though he's not talking to me, I gulp. A band of fear tightens across my chest. Kyle struggles up the last step just as Mom steps onto the porch.

Mom's voice is low, but I can hear the tension in it. "Your mother and Aunt Sarah are in the kitchen. Lock the door behind you." She pushes Kyle through the door. "Go inside. Now."

Mom glances at the three of us, huddled behind the Chevy, and motions "stay" with her hand. She throws her shoulders back, turns to face the driver, and walks towards the limo. The driver towers over her. He pulls off his sunglasses so she can get the full benefit of his menacing glare. Mom takes another step towards him and then stops with her feet planted shoulder width apart and arms loose at her sides.

I can't help the smirk on my face. My mom might only be five feet tall, but she's an expert in both Judo and Jujitsu. She's the reason I've got a green belt. Hers is black. Yeah, she's that good. I've seen her throw men almost as big as this guy over her shoulder and pin them to the ground before they ever saw it coming.

Trey whispers in my ear, "I wish I could hear what she's saying."

Alex nodded. "They have no idea who they're messing with."

It's true. My mom is something of a legend in our little part of the world. She teaches Judo back home and she used to compete in tournaments when I was a little kid. I've seen her in action. She's good. But these guys are pretty scary.

Just then, a tall, slender woman with a tornado of short white hair stomps across the lawn. She puts a protective arm around Mom and matches the driver's glare with a fierce one of her own. "I told you before that this property is not for sale. Not for any price. Now get off my land before I call the sheriff."

That's my Great Aunt Sarah; recently retired missionary, and owner of a peach orchard in Palisade, Colorado.

Chapter 2

Aunt Sarah turns to us and barks, "Alex, Brandon, Trey. To the house. Call 911 if these clowns aren't off my property in thirty seconds."

We scamper across the lawn and onto the porch. The peeling paint and rickety railing on the looming, two-story house seemed a little creepy a minute ago. But now, this tattered old house with its banging shutters and uneven steps is totally my safe zone.

Aunt Bekki throws the door open, and we all try to shove through the door at the same time, like a scene in a cartoon. Aunt Bekki grabs Trey's arm and pulls him into the entryway. Alex and I tumble onto the marble tiles after him. My heart is thumping in my ears, and I feel like I ran a mile instead of a quick sprint across the lawn.

We all turn and press our faces against the window beside the fancy carved door. Mom and Aunt Sarah just look like dark blobs through the leaded glass. Aunt Bekki cracks the front door open, and we peek over each other's shoulders in a staggered line; Alex, Aunt Bekki, Kyle, me, and then Trey on the bottom. I would think it's funny if I wasn't so freaked out.

"What are they saying?" Alex asks.

I was wondering the same thing.

"I can't hear them." Aunt Bekki is chewing her bottom lip and her face is the color of chalk. *I'm not the only one that thinks this is scary.* "It makes me think of David and Goliath." With a grin, she adds, "I was thinking of your mom as David, not as the giant."

Across the lawn, Aunt Sarah is shaking her finger at the enormous man as though he's a naughty schoolboy. He puts his sunglasses on and then gets behind the wheel of the Suburban. The rear window glides closed, and I can see Aunt Sarah's frown reflected in the dark-tinted glass. The engine roars and gravel spits against our green Jeep as the Suburban churns across the driveway. Aunt Sarah and Mom stand shoulder to shoulder until the vehicle disappears around the bend in the road.

I guess we don't have to call 911.

I've only been to Aunt Sarah's house once before. Waiting for Mom and Aunt Sarah to join us, I glance around. The place is huge. We're standing in an entry hall with white marble floors and a ceiling so high it reminds me of a museum. There's a huge stairway curving to the right with a carved eagle at the bottom of the railing. The walls are covered with paintings.

To my left is a room with old-fashioned furniture. I take a step towards the room and peek inside. *Maybe I should pay admission before I go any further.* It looks *just* like a museum. Thick curtains are pulled closed, blocking any sunlight that might dare to sneak in, and a thick floral rug covers most of the marble floor. A carved white fireplace fills the center wall and I can just make out a grand piano in one corner.

"Well." Aunt Sarah's voice pulls my attention back to the entry hall. The sunlight that streams from the stairway window shines through her hair, giving her a halo. She winks a sparkling blue eye. "That's one way to make a memorable beginning."

Mom sighs and runs her fingers through her much longer, much darker hair. Her coffee-colored eyes are shadowed with concern, and I don't see any indication of winking. When her eyes meet mine, she smiles, but I'm not convinced she means it.

"Jennifer, stop worrying." Aunt Sarah rubs Mom's shoulder with an age-spotted hand. "It's all under control."

"I don't know." Aunt Bekki is chewing her lip again. "I can cancel my trip. It's just a seminar."

"A seminar you've been looking forward to attending." Aunt Sarah is taller than Mom and Aunt Bekki, and she puts her arms around their shoulders. "We're going ahead with things as planned." She gives Aunt Bekki a stern look. "Bek, you're going to that seminar in Atlanta and learn all about … whatever it is you do with those computers. I'll never understand what exactly you do, but I know you're very good at it."

Aunt Sarah turns to Mom with the don't-argue expression that Mom uses on me. *Maybe that's where Mom learned it!* "Jennifer, you go back to Lake City and take care of those guests. You've got a resort full of Girl Scouts and that's more than enough on your shoulders."

Aunt Sarah looks at the four of us. Alex is slumped against the wall, staring at his cell phone with a scowl on his face. Trey and Kyle are standing next to me, and I can't help but think we all look a little scared. Alex is trying to cover with his moody-teen pose, but the chalk-white color of his face doesn't do much to convince me.

"We'll be fine, won't we boys?" Aunt Sarah's eyebrows lift in expectation.

"Great." Kyle says a little too loudly. *If he says it loud enough, maybe he'll believe it himself.*

Trey chirps in with, "Yeah, we'll be fine." *Also, not convincing.*

I'm mesmerized by the pattern of crevices and lines in Aunt Sarah's forehead, and almost forget to add my own, "Yeah, sure."

Mom gives me the one-eyebrow-lift look that says she doesn't believe a word of it.

Aunt Sarah claps her hands. "Perfect. That's settled. Now, Jennifer, you'd best get going." She glances at the enormous grandfather clock ticking in the corner beside the stairs. "Bek has a plane to catch."

"Oh!" Aunt Bekki looks at the clock. "I was going to call my friend and have her come get the car. I'm not sure if I have time…"

Aunt Sarah waves her hand as if she's shooing away a fly. "We can park it in the carriage house. When Dan gets back in town, he can pick it up."

Dan, that's my uncle. Kyle's dad. He travels a lot for his work.

"Well… if you're sure it's not in your way." Aunt Bekki gives Aunt Sarah another uncertain glance. "Dan won't be back until Friday."

Aunt Sarah pats her niece on the back. "It's fine. I have plenty of room."

With a relieved smile, Aunt Bekki bends down to hug Kyle. "And you, mister." Aunt Bekki's eyes fill with tears as she wraps her arms around her son. "I'm going to miss you."

"Have a good seminar, Mom. Learn all the new technology." Kyle's voice is muffled by his mom's hug. When she pulls away, his grin is like that cat in the cartoon. "Then you can teach it to me."

Aunt Bekki raises her eyebrows and gives Kyle a pretend-worried look. "You scare me, kid." By the smile she gives him, I can tell she's proud of her computer-geek son.

I try not to be jealous of the cell phone she presses into Kyle's hand. "Like we talked about, daytime use only. No staying up all night playing games. And Aunt Sarah is the boss of your phone use. Got it?"

"Thanks, Mom." Kyle gives her a salute. "I promise to use it only for good and not for evil."

Aunt Bekki rolls her eyes and messes up his hair. "I knew I could count on you, Captain Kyle. Dismissed." The tears glistening in the corner of her eyes don't match the playful tone of her voice.

Mom squeezes me tight and whispers "I'll miss you." But, as much as I wish for it, she doesn't press a cell phone into my hands. Our family has strict rules about cell phones and 16th birthdays. Mom and Dad don't seem to know what century this is.

Trey blinks back tears as Aunt Bekki and Mom drive away. He's only ten, after all. And a month without Mom or Dad *does* seem like a long time.

Just then, I notice a black cat sitting on the stairs, looking at us with his head tilted to the side as if he's sizing us up. He's got a white spot on his mouth like he forgot to wipe the milk off his lips, and a white patch on his chest. Moving slowly, I let him sniff my fingers before reaching for his silky head. He doesn't pull away when I touch his ears, so I run my hand along his back and over his tail.

"I see you've met Chester." Aunt Sarah sits down on a stair step and Chester chirrs a greeting. "Chester, this is Brandon. He's going to be staying with us for the next month or so."

"Hey Chester." I scratch the fur behind his ear, and he cranks out a purr that could rattle the windows. "You like that, huh?" The next thing I know, Chester is sitting in my lap and rubbing his big head across my hand. His rumbling purr echoes across the room.

Kyle and Trey come to say hello, and the cat greets them with the chirring sound and then ratchets up the purr another decibel.

"He's so cool."

Chester blinks his luminous green eyes at me as if to say, "Thanks."

Kyle and Trey laugh as the cat lifts a paw like he wants to shake, and I swear he smiles. Even Alex can't resist the purring, smiling cat, and soon he's running his hand over Chester's sleek back.

"It's going to be time for dinner soon," Aunt Sarah interrupts our cat-adoration session. "Would you rather order pizza, or should we go into town for dinner?"

I glance at the others. Alex just shrugs and Kyle and Trey give me blank stares. "I've had enough of riding in the car for one day. Do you mind if we order pizza?" I hope it's okay if I speak for the group, but nobody else is saying anything.

"Sounds reasonable to me." Aunt Sarah pulls a phone from the pocket of her long skirt. "What kind of pizza do you boys like? I'm getting one with everything. What should I get for the rest of you?"

After a discussion on the merits of pepperoni vs. ham and Kyle turning up his nose at vegetables on pizza, Aunt Sarah orders a large thick-crust double-pepperoni, a large thick-crust supreme, a large hand-tossed crust ham-and-pineapple and something called The Geek. That seems like a lot of pizza, even to me.

"Now," Aunt Sarah says to the person taking our order, "if you could send those out with Emily when she gets off shift, that would be lovely." She gives them her credit card info and disconnects with a smile. "Dinner will be here in about an hour. And you'll get to meet Emily."

Alex reestablishes his slumped position against the wall. "Who's Emily?"

"She and her father live in one of the guest houses. Her dad helps me run the orchard and Emily is helping with some of my other projects."

Alex nods, like he doesn't really care, and scrolls through the newsfeed on his phone. But his eyes light up when Aunt Sarah adds one last bit of information.

"She just finished her junior year of high school. She's working at Diorio's Pizza in Palisade for the summer."

"You have guest houses?" Kyle asks. "This place must be huge."

"Well, guest houses might be a generous term," Aunt Sarah says with a sigh. "They need a lot of work. They've been used as housing for the migrant workers for the past few years. The man who was managing the orchard didn't do much in the way of upkeep. But, come along. I'll give you the grand tour." Aunt Sarah pops up from the stairs and smooths her skirt. Her brown leather sandals make a clop-clop sound on the floor.

I set Chester down and follow Aunt Sarah outside. Chester trots along behind. I guess he's coming, too.

Chapter 3

Aunt Sarah tosses a set of keys to Alex. "Would you pull Bek's Chevy into the carriage house for me, please?" She lopes across the drive and heads towards a building half-hidden behind a lilac bush overflowing with purple blossoms. "You can park it next to the side-by-side."

"What's a side-by-side?" Trey asks.

Aunt Sarah answers over her shoulder. "It's a type of four-wheeler. The orchard has a few ATV's. The side-by-side is bigger, so the four of us can ride together. Alex, you can follow us on one of the other four-wheelers, and we'll tour the property while we're waiting for our pizza."

Kyle bumps Trey with his hip. "Dad let me drive Aunt Sarah's side-by-side last time we were here."

Trey eyes Kyle to see if he's messing with us. "Really?"

Kyle nods and throws his chest out. "Yeah, for real."

Aunt Sarah pulls the double-doors of the carriage house open to reveal a red and black side-by-side and two matching four-wheelers. The space inside is dark, but I can make out another shape in the shadowed interior. It looks like a military vehicle.

"What's that?" I press past Trey and Kyle as they stroke the surfaces of the ATV's. Aunt Sarah stands beside me, and we pause to watch Alex ease the Chevy into the empty space beside the ATV's.

"This is a 1977 Series 3 Land Rover." Aunt Sarah pats a dingy green fender. "This old girl is a treasure. Seats seven, and in pretty good shape for her age." Her eyes take on a misty, far-away look. "We had one almost like this in Colombia. Joe and I had a lot of adventures in that old thing." Aunt Sarah snaps her attention back to me and says, "She runs, but needs a little work. I haven't gotten around to finding someone to fix up the old girl."

"It has a spare tire on the hood," I blurt out.

"Yeah." Aunt Sarah taps the tire, and her eyes get that misty look again. "It's handy to have a spare tire close at hand when you're in the jungle."

Trey has lost interest in the ATV's and is now studying the Land Rover. "This is a peach orchard, not a jungle."

"True." Aunt Sarah nods. "I don't know how the peach orchard ended up with a Land Rover, or when." She shrugs. "It was here when I got here."

Chester hops onto the hood of the Land Rover and sniffs the tire. He rubs against my hand and his deep, throaty purr rumbles through the carriage house. Aunt Sarah rubs his ear. "And this guy joined me soon after I arrived. You'd never dream he was such a scrawny little thing that I didn't think he'd survive."

I laugh. "Scrawny, huh? He's the biggest cat I've ever seen." Chester pauses to lick a giant paw and then pushes his head against my hand for more ear scratching.

Alex has finished parking the Chevy and is standing next to me. "How long have you owned this orchard?"

I'm wondering the same thing. This place seems kind of fancy for a missionary.

Aunt Sarah gets behind the wheel of the side-by-side and motions for us to join her. "This orchard and the surrounding property belonged to my husband's family. That would be your Great Uncle Joe. His grandfather, who was your great-great something or other, built the house back in the 1920's. Joe inherited this place when his father died. We were in Colombia at the time, so we hired someone to manage the property. We always planned to retire here." She starts the engine of the ATV. "Joe died about a year ago, and I... I came to Palisade like we'd planned. I just never dreamed it would be without your

Uncle Joe." She clears her throat and revs the engine. "Hop in, boys."

I jump into the back seat of the side-by-side and grab onto the red bar of the roll cage. Kyle climbs in beside me while Trey clambers into the front seat. Aunt Sarah turns her head to make sure Alex was able to start the other ATV. He gives her a thumbs up as Chester hops into the side-by-side and settles in my lap. With ATV's rumbling, we pull onto the driveway. I blink as the bright afternoon sunlight hits my face.

The air is heavy with the scent of ripening peaches. I close my eyes and breathe deeply. My eyes pop open in surprise as Chester's claws dig into my thighs when we round a corner. "Ow, buddy. Ease up, there. I won't let you fall out." I pry a needle-sharp claw out of my leg.

Aunt Sarah glances over her shoulder. "Oh, Chester. I didn't realize you'd joined us." She turns back to the front of the vehicle. "That silly cat loves to go for rides."

"This row has Early Red Haven peaches. They'll be ready to harvest in about a month. Mid-July. Over there, we've got Belair's." I study the tidy rows of trees and the green globes tucked behind the leaves. *How can she tell what kind of peaches they are? They all look exactly the same to me.*

As we bounce between another row of trees, we come across two men in jeans and long-sleeved shirts spraying something on the leaves of the peach trees. Aunt Sarah lifts a hand in greeting and they pause what they're doing to wave back. The flash of white teeth against the weathered faces, and the way their dark eyes follow us with curious interest makes me feel like they're genuinely happy to see us.

After jolting across a few more rows of trees, Aunt Sarah pulls the ATV to the side and motions for Alex to pull alongside. An enormous cottonwood tree with branches that tangle into a heart-shape towers over us. Aunt Sarah climbs out of the vehicle, and we scramble after her. Alex kills the motor on his four-wheeler and swings his leg over the seat. We stand beside Aunt Sarah as she points across a valley.

"Those are the Bookcliffs." She points to the weird, moon-scape cliffs that tower in the distance. "They actually provide radiant heat to the orchards, making this a good climate for growing peaches. And grapes." She points to another spot in the distance. "There are several vineyards too. You can see the Jones place over there. They have about ten acres, I think." We stare across the valley at the rugged stone cliffs of Mount Garfield, the lush rows of green trees and well-tended grapevines, the brilliant blue sky. I can see a white fence that encloses four horses in a triangle-shaped pasture and the red-tiled roofs of what must be the Jones place.

"Wow." I don't have any other words to describe how this makes me feel. I mean, we live in a cool place too, with mountains and blue sky all around. But the scene spread below us here is a different kind of beautiful. I want to soak it in and remember it forever.

Aunt Sarah smiles at me. "I know what you mean." We stand in silence for a few more minutes before Aunt Sarah urges us back to the ATV's. We rumble and bounce along for another few minutes. Chester sniffs the air with his head out the side and the breeze rippling his fur, and I wince every time his claws jab into my thigh. But I'm holding onto the red grab-bar as we swerve around the corners, so I understand his need for stability.

We stop again in front of a row of four tiny houses. What remains of the once-white paint hangs in tattered strips from weathered siding. The jumble of red, brown and green shingles on top of each house reminds me of an ugly quilt. Bare wood peeks through the multi-colored layers in a few spots. The house on the end has curtains in the windows and a couple of chairs set on the sagging front porch. I can see an outhouse in the back, with a well-worn path through the ankle-high grass.

"Does someone actually live here?" I can't keep the shock from my voice.

"Yep. Emily and her father, Stan." Aunt Sarah doesn't seem phased by my question. "Stan is my right-hand man." She smiles at the slightly awkward rhyme. "We had to fix the septic system, so the plumbing is shut off at the moment, but the electric system and wiring have been upgraded. We're pretty busy with the orchard right now, but Stan is helping me get these little houses fixed up so I can use them as Airbnb rentals." She spreads her arms wide and turns in a circle. "I think people would pay to stay here, don't you?"

"Yeah, I guess." I mutter my half-hearted agreement. "But talk about your fixer-uppers." *An outhouse? Really?*

Kyle's face is scrunched up like he can smell the outhouse. "You're going to have electricity, though, right? And you'll need dependable wifi. If guests can't download the pictures they took that day, or stream a movie after a day of biking, they're not gonna give you good reviews. And reviews are important for an Airbnb."

Alex thumps the back of Kyle's head. "Geez, Kyle. That is seriously rude! I suppose you're an expert on Airbnb's now too?"

Kyle rubs the back of his head and moves away from Alex. "A lot of people in Palisade have part-time rentals. I hear things!"

Aunt Sarah swats Alex's hand with a laugh. "Kyle wasn't being rude. Blunt, maybe." She tips her head to one side and studies the tattered little houses. "But let's face it, I'm an old lady who's lived in a third world country for a *looong* time." She draws out the word long and makes an emoji-face. "I need to know about these things. Good information, Kyle. Thanks."

As we load back into the ATV's, I spot an outdoor shower set up on the back side of the little house. I used one of those on a camping trip with Dad. A shiver runs through my entire body at the memory. *Poor Stan. I hope he gets the plumbing fixed before the end of summer.*

We head back at a speed that has me gripping the padded red bar like my life depends on it. I breathe a sigh of extreme relief when the towering pines and not-quite-peeling paint of the big gray house comes into view. It seems like a mansion compared to the ragged, little houses we left behind. Actually, it seems like a mansion compared to most houses. A worn-out, tired mansion. But still.

The tires crunch to a stop in the circular driveway and I release my white-knuckled grip on the padded cage that surrounds the vehicle. Then I peel Chester's claws from my leg. Now I see why Aunt Sarah needs a roll bar. *Yikes.*

A blue sedan is parked in the driveway. Aunt Sarah shouts over her shoulder, "Emily is here with the pizza!"

Aunt Sarah parks the side-by-side and turns to me. "Brandon, would you lock up the carriage house? I don't usually worry about it, but this nonsense with the visitors this afternoon has me a little edgy."

While she greets Emily, Trey and I swing the double doors closed and shove the chain through the long, cast-iron handles. I snap the lock and jiggle it to make sure it's tight.

"Wait! Where's the cat?" Trey asks as he looks around.

"Oh no! I didn't look to see if he came out. Chester? Chester!"

Chester saunters into the sunlight from beneath the overgrown lilac bush and plops down in front of us. He rubs a paw over the white spot on his chin and then yawns, showing us his pink tongue and sharp, white teeth. I scoop Chester up and bring him with us to the house. It takes both arms and a bit of effort to carry the giant cat.

The door to the house is open but everyone's hovering on the porch. Aunt Sarah holds a tower of pizza boxes and the smell wafts across the lawn, making my stomach rumble. Alex is talking to a petite, dark-haired girl that I assume is Emily.

Kyle charges across the gravel until he's standing in front of us and then walks backwards as we head to the house. "Did you see the horse?"

I stare at Kyle in confusion. Trey gives me a puzzled look and shrugs his shoulders. I adjust the cat in my arms and shake my head. "Uh, no. We closed the doors on the carriage house and picked up the cat. No horses."

"What did we miss?" Trey looks around the yard. "We were only gone a minute."

"There's a horse, a big brown one. It was eating Aunt Sarah's front lawn and when we walked up, it bolted into the orchard. Aunt Sarah is calling the neighbors."

I crane my neck to see if I can spot the rogue horse in the orchard. The sun is low in the sky, and the late afternoon shadows make it hard to see between the well-tended trees. I know from experience that an ornery horse could take a while to catch. I sigh and set Chester down on the porch steps.

"Don't look so worried, kid." Alex pats my shoulder as I walk past him and the stunningly pretty girl on the porch. "I've already volunteered to catch the horse and take it back to his owners. Emily's going to help me."

The girl flashes a dazzling-white smile at me and stretches out her hand. "Hi. I'm Emily."

Taking her hand, I look into her face, and …can't remember what I'm supposed to do next. Her almond-shaped eyes are fringed by long, thick lashes. No make-up. Just gorgeous, toffee-colored skin and a killer smile. I drop her hand, realizing that I've been holding it too long. "Uh, yeah. Nice to meet you." I manage to stammer out the words and then bolt into the house.

My face burns as I hear Alex laugh. "That's my brother, Brandon. He's a charmer."

Emily's voice has a scolding tone. "Don't tease him. He's just shy."

"Hey, are we gonna eat or what?" Kyle demands. I'm relieved when everyone's attention shifts to the boxes on the kitchen table.

Aunt Sarah has laid out paper plates and napkins over a blue-checked tablecloth. A pitcher of lemonade and a pitcher of ice water sit on the counter, condensation trickling down the sides and leaving wet rings on the chipped plastic countertop.

We wash our hands in the kitchen and it takes me a minute to figure out how to turn the old-fashioned knobs. Cold is on one side, and hot on the other; I have to choose which stream of water to dip my hands into. Trails of ancient mineral residue beneath each faucet line the deep, porcelain sink.

The pizza is amazing. With ravenous hunger fueling my choices, I try the one called The Greek. Kyle won't even consider it because it has spinach and tomatoes, along with pepperoni and all kinds of other stuff. *Ha! More for me.*

After I eat so much I can hardly wiggle, Aunt Sarah pulls a cheesecake from her refrigerator. Oh no. If I'd known there was cheesecake, I wouldn't have eaten that last piece of pizza. *Well, maybe.*

Alex and Emily excuse themselves and head out to look for the neighbor's horse. His name is Oscar, and I guess this isn't the first time old Oscar has gone wandering. Even though Aunt Sarah doesn't have any horses of her own, she has a lead and harness in the carriage house. For Oscar. And his often-roaming pasture buddies.

We stuff ourselves on cheesecake – with strawberries and whipped cream – yum! and then I help Aunt Sarah put the leftover pizza away. There's not much to put away. We were pretty hungry.

"How long have you lived here?" I ask as I put three slices of ham-and-pineapple in a baggie and tug on the plastic zipper. We ate a lot of pizza, but there's still plenty left for Alex and Emily.

Aunt Sarah gazes at the ceiling, as if the answer is in the water-stained plaster above our heads. "About nine months. I came here right after Joe died."

I'm not sure what to say. I didn't really know Uncle Joe, so I'm not sad about him dying, but it's awkward just the same. I can tell Aunt Sarah misses him because whenever she says his name, she gets that watery, far-away look in her eyes.

"That must have been hard." I chew my lip. "I mean, it must still be hard, to be here, retired like you planned, but he's not…you know. Here."

She gives me a sideways glance and then nods her head. "You're right. Not what I had hoped for or planned. And I do miss him." She turns to look at me head on. "Which is one of the reasons I twisted your mom's arm into letting you stay with me. I am really looking forward to a month of some life in this old mausoleum."

Chapter 4

The pizza is put away, the paper plates and plastic cups shoved in the trash. I volunteer to take the overflowing kitchen trash to the bin beside the carriage house. Rain is pounding down, and I'm soaked from the sprint.

As I'm wiping my muddy feet on the rug by the kitchen door, Aunt Sarah's phone rings. It's Mom. *She'll be proud of me for remembering to wipe my feet. Nah, I won't mention it.* But I feel good about my secret thoughtfulness. Aunt Sarah hands me the phone.

"Hey kiddo." At the sound of Mom's voice, tears threaten to bubble up from deep inside. "How's it going so far?"

"Good." I swallow the lump in my throat. "We got to ride in a side-by-side. It's really pretty here."

"I know," Mom says. "I spent time there when I was your age. Of course, we didn't have ATV's. We had to walk!" Her laugh echoes through the kitchen.

"Did you make it home okay?"

"Yep. I'm home. And the Girl Scouts will be here in the morning, so you know… all the last-minute stuff tonight."

I did know. Mom would check all the rooms to make sure they were stocked with toilet paper and soap, beds made to her standards. Then she would spend time in the commercial-sized kitchen to make sure meal-prep for the hungry campers was completed. Meanwhile, Dad would be doing final preparations on the activities-end of things; horseback riding, zip-lines, canoe trips and leather crafts. They'd both stay up late tonight and then be up at the crack of dawn. It takes a lot of behind-the-scenes work to run a mountain retreat center.

"Okay, well don't stay up all night, Mom." I know she will, but I say it anyway.

Mom laughs again. "I'll try to get to bed at a reasonable time if you will." Her voice softens. "I love you, Brandon."

"Love you too." My voice catches on the words. "Here's Trey." I shove the phone into his hands and turn away so he can't see me rub my leaky eyes with the back of my hand.

Trey tells Mom about Oscar the horse and that Alex is showing off for Emily at this very moment with his horse-wrangling skills. *Trey's right, that's exactly what Alex is doing*. After a few minutes, Trey tells Mom goodbye, hands the phone back to Aunt Sarah and bolts from the room. Nobody mentions his red-rimmed eyes when he walks back in a few minutes later.

"How about some music?" Aunt Sarah leads us into the museum-room with the marble fireplace and the giant piano. She fumbles along the wall until she finds a light switch.

"Whoa." Trey and Kyle stop in the middle of the room, heads swiveling in all directions as they take it all in. "This is amazing." Kyle touches the detailed carving on the stone fireplace.

"Amazing is one word for it." Aunt Sarah rolls her eyes. "Mausoleum is the word that comes to *my* mind."

"Mahzo what?" Trey scrunches his nose as he asks.

"Mausoleum," Aunt Sarah repeats. "It means a fancy place for dead things." She bends over and rolls the floral rug into a giant tube, revealing marble tiles that glisten in the soft glow of the overhead light. My eyes travel upwards, and I let out a low whistle at the chandelier dangling above our heads.

"Now then," Aunt Sarah grabs the side of a blue curve-backed sofa. "Brandon, grab this end, will you?"

We scoot the sofa against the wall and move a couple of heavy, dark wood tables in place beside it. Aunt Sarah sits down at the piano and runs her fingers against the keys, filling the room with a cheerful crescendo. My eyes open in shock when the opening bars of an Elvis Presley song flood the room.

When Alex wanders into the room, we're dancing to *Jail House Rock* as Aunt Sarah pounds the piano and belts out the words to the song. When she shoved that stool across the room so she could bang the keys a little harder, we just *had* to dance. Not that I know how to dance, but that somehow doesn't matter.

Alex is in his stocking feet and dripping wet. I had forgotten about the rain pounding against the house and the wind whistling through the trees. And here we are, having fun, while he was out in the storm.

Alex's expression is a mixture of shock and amusement. "Looks like I missed the party." He shakes his head and raises one eyebrow. "Aunt Sarah, that was impressive." He flashes a genuine smile. "Really cool."

I wonder how old she is, this mystery we call Aunt Sarah; the whirlwind of white hair, the fan of fine lines around her eyes and the deep creases in her forehead, the ready-to-laugh twinkle in her bright, blue eyes. And I've never, ever heard anyone play the piano like this.

When we finally tromp up the stairs towards our bedrooms, I'm ready. It's been a long day and I'm looking forward to a chance to stretch out. Aunt Sarah shows Kyle, Trey and I to our rooms, with enormous beds and a bathroom down the hall. We brush our teeth and then go to our separate rooms to do all the usual bedtime things.

Pulling pajamas from my suitcase, I slip them over my head just as the wind whips a shutter against the side of the house. I almost strangle myself with a sleeve. *Wow, this old house has a lot of creaks and groans.* I wrestle the shirt over my head and open the bedroom door. It's nice to have my own room but I'm used to having Trey underfoot, and it feels a little weird without him. Trey and Kyle are in rooms across the hallway. I didn't even think to ask where Alex is sleeping. He didn't follow us up the stairs, so I guess he's downstairs somewhere. *This place is huge. I wonder how many bedrooms there are?*

Aunt Sarah hovers in the doorway and whispers goodnight as I snuggle into the soft-as-hoped-for bed. The hall light goes out, and a soft glow comes from the thoughtfully placed nightlight beside the dresser. The house creaks and groans, as if it's settling in for the night, too.

The dark spot above the bed looks like the state of Idaho. I have a wooden puzzle of the United States at home, and that's the exact shape of the Idaho piece. Chester hops onto the bed and nudges my hand. Just as I reach out to stroke his silky back, a figure appears beside the bed.

It takes a second for my heart to beat again. *It's only Trey.*

"Come on," I grumble, flipping the blankets aside. I don't really mind that Trey slips in beside me. He's only ten, after all. And this is a creaky, old house.

I mind a little more when Kyle slips in on the other side a few minutes later. His legs are so long, they push the blankets out at the bottom and cool air brushes my toes. But the bed is big and soft. And it's been a long day. I tug the blanket back over my feet and close my eyes. Chester's soothing purr lulls me to sleep.

Chapter 5

I wake with a startle, my heart pounding. A crushing weight pins my legs to the mattress. *I can't move! Where am I?* A low rumble vibrates against my shins. *Chester.*

I sit up and try to shove the enormous fur-ball off my legs. Kyle and Trey are wedged against me on either side. I feel like the black beans in a burrito at Chipotle.

With a determined shove, I roll Chester onto the mattress. I'm pushing Trey's drooling face off my pillow when I hear a crash. Right outside the bedroom. *What was that?* My own frantic heartbeat drowns out all other sounds.

Trey's eyes are open when I glance down. Wide with fear. He heard it too.

Chester moves to the foot of the bed, his ears down, a low growl rumbling from his tense body. He leaps from the bed to investigate.

That's a brave cat. I can't move.

"What was that?" Trey's whisper seems to echo in the shadowy room.

Just then, another crash is followed by a high-pitched yowl. Adrenaline surges through my body and, finally unfrozen, I bolt from the bed. I bound into the hallway just in time to see Chester leap through the window.

The long, narrow window at the end of the hallway is broken, letting a blast of rain-tinged air into the hallway. Wind whips through the room, snagging lace curtains on shattered glass. The little table by the window is laying on the floor, with pieces of a pottery jug scattered across the rug. Two smaller jugs roll from side to side with every gust of air.

Tiptoeing over the shards of pottery, I peer out the second-story window. "Oh, whew." A gable that shelters the kitchen window on the ground level of the house has given Chester a launchpad to the muddy yard below.

Searching the darkness for the mostly-black cat, my eyes are drawn to movement. But that's not Chester! Lightning flashes across the sky just as a man wearing a hooded jacket lunges into the backseat of a dark SUV. The vehicle's engine roars and gravel sprays beneath the tires as it disappears into the blackness.

I feel a hand on my shoulder and jump about a foot in the air, squeaking like a panicked mouse. With my hand over my pounding heart like I'm trying to keep it from leaping out of my chest, I turn.

Aunt' Sarah's face is ashy-white in the glow from the nightlight. "Are you all right?" Her frown deepens as she looks over my shoulder and across the rain-soaked lawn. "Did anyone hurt you?"

"I'm okay. I saw someone running away but they weren't in the house." I pause, considering the crash and Chester's heroic leap from the window. "I didn't *see* them in the house," I correct my statement.

Aunt Sarah nudges me away from the window. "I don't want to alarm you, but..." she points to a set of muddy footprints on the hardwood floor. "There *was* someone in the house. I've called 911." She wraps me in a hug so tight I can barely breathe. "The sheriff's department should be here soon." Trey and Kyle stand like wide-eyed statues against the wall. She repeats the lung-crushing hugs with them before she herds us downstairs to wait.

Before following Kyle downstairs, I glance at the hallway. *What a mess.*

My teeth chatter, even though I'm not cold. Scrunched on the couch between Kyle and Trey, I listen to the clatter of dishes in the kitchen. Even Alex is quiet, perching on the footstool with his chin in his hand.

A few minutes later, Aunt Sarah covers me with a crocheted afghan and shoves a cup of hot chocolate into my hands. She does the same for Trey, Kyle and Alex.

"I think I hear Chester," Kyle announces, hope flickering in his brown eyes.

With a frown, Alex pushes up from his position on the foot stool. "I doubt it. He jumped from a second story window."

"He jumped onto the thingy over the kitchen door, and then to the ground." Kyle chews his fingernail. "So maybe he's okay, right?"

"I'll go look." Alex rolls his eyes. "But don't get your hopes up."

A few moments later the cat walks into the room with his tail in a giant question mark. Alex grins as he follows the cat. "You were right, Kyle. Other than being a little wet, he looks okay."

"Chester!" Kyle shoves his cup into my hand, drops his afghan and lunges towards the cat. Chester shakes a wet paw and meows. We all laugh, relief washing through us.

The doorbell rings a few minutes later and two deputies with serious faces join our group. They don't look much older than Alex.

The blond deputy takes charge of the room. "Hello, boys, ma'am. I'm Deputy Pelton with Mesa County Sheriff's Department. This is Deputy Chavez." He points to the man beside him. "Is everyone okay? Do we need to call for medical help?"

Aunt Sarah shakes her head. "We're frightened, but no one is injured."

"I'm glad to hear that. We'll do our best to catch this guy. Any details you can give us about what happened could be helpful."

The next few minutes are a jumble of voices. We talk over each other, trying to put events into words. I tell them about Chester leaping out the window, the guy in the jacket, and the SUV driving away without lights. Aunt Sarah tells them about the incident earlier in the afternoon.

"Nothing is missing?" The deputy with blond hair glances at Aunt Sarah for confirmation.

"I took a quick look around before you arrived. I'm not sure. I think one of my pottery jugs is missing."

"A pottery jug. Is it valuable?"

"Only to me." Aunt Sarah rubs her face with a shaking hand. "They were gifts from my kids." She blinks away a tear. "The children made sweets and hand-made jewelry for my going-away celebration. One of the boys gave me some pottery jugs." She sighs. "You can find one just like it in any market in Colombia."

"Mrs. Hooper do you believe the incident this afternoon and the break-in tonight are connected?" The deputy scribbles something on a little form and waits for her answer with raised eyebrows.

Aunt Sarah's eyes flash in irritation and she squints at his name tag "Yes, Deputy Pelton, I do." Her icy tone suggests that only an idiot would not see the connection. Then her face softens, and she tips her head to the side. "E. Pelton," Aunt Sarah repeats the name engraved on the pin of his uniform. "As in, Larry and Shirley Pelton's boy, Eric?"

"Yes ma'am." He smiles. "My parents still live in the old house where I grew up."

"Yes, a beautiful Victorian house in Palisade." Aunt Sarah's tone is much kinder this time. "I've known your parents for years. They were faithful supporters of our ministry in Colombia."

Deputy Pelton's smile gets a little bigger. "Mom always kept a picture of your kids on our refrigerator."

"Your kids?" Trey asks with a puzzled frown. "I didn't think you had any kids."

Aunt Sarah shrugs her shoulders. "Well, not children that I gave birth to, no. But Joe and I raised a few children in Colombia."

The deputy laughs. "A few. Mom still has the last Christmas card you sent from Colombia on the fridge. I think there's close to thirty kids in that picture."

Aunt Sarah's eyes get that far-away look. "We had thirty-two children under our care before Joe's illness." She sighs and closes her eyes. "That was the hardest part about leaving." Aunt Sarah takes a deep breath and blinks away a tear. "But back to the matter at hand. Perhaps you would like to see the muddy footprints?"

Deputy Chavez nods. "Lead the way, Mrs. Hooper."

We traipse behind them, but Aunt Sarah motions for us to stop at the curved archway leading into the kitchen. She points out a large print beside the kitchen door, then to three muddy blobs across the kitchen floor, and another at the foot of the stairs. *Now I'm really glad I remembered to wipe my feet!*

Alex's face pales. He whispers, "I think I bumped into that guy at the bottom of the stairs."

"What?" Aunt Sarah and both deputies say it at the same time.

Alex leads them back to the entry area and points to a door beside the giant curved stairs. "I came upstairs for some leftover pizza, and I brushed against something in the dark. I thought…" He points to the carved eagle at the bottom of the stairs. "I thought I bumped into this." His Adam's apple bobs, and his face goes another shade lighter. "I thought someone hung a jacket over the eagle. All I was thinking about was pizza…"

"Okay." Deputy Pelton flips open his notebook and jots down a few words. "Walk me through what happened next."

Alex points at the stairs. "I heard a crash and then I heard someone running down the stairs." Alex looks at me and his face turns red. "I thought it was Brandon messing around. When the guy ran out the front door, I realized it wasn't Brandon." He shoots me an apology with his eyes. "The guy jumped into a big SUV. I think it was the Suburban from earlier today."

Deputy Pelton nods. "You're sure it was a man?" Alex nods. I nod. We look like a trio of bobble-heads.

"You both saw a man in a hooded jacket get into a dark SUV. The vehicle did not have lights on. Correct?"

"Correct," Alex says. "No lights. But when he opened the door, I could see the size and shape of the vehicle."

"Yeah, me too." My head bobs up and down as I blurt out the memory, "The light came on when he opened the door. But there was a flash of lightning at the same time." I put my hands on my neck. *Stop nodding!*

I try to shove away the image of the three of us as bobble-head dolls, but I can't control a snort of hard-to-explain laughter.

Aunt Sarah gives me a concerned glance as she leads the group up the stairs. I hang back, touching the smooth, glossy surface of the eagle and picturing where the man must have been standing when Alex bumped into him. With a shiver, I race up the stairs.

Just as my foot hits the landing, the doorbell rings. I can't see the front door from this position, but I hear the door open, and a man's voice calls out, "Sarah? Are you okay?"

I press against the wall as Aunt Sarah rushes down the stairs. "Stan. Thank God you're here."

Creeping down a couple of steps, I pause, uncertain if I should go up or down. Now I can see the front entry, and Aunt Sarah is hugging a stocky man with dark hair.

"Where's Emily?" The concern in her voice spikes my heart rate. Padding the rest of the way down the stairs, I hover beside the carved eagle as Aunt Sarah steps onto the porch. A minute later she comes back in with Emily in tow. Emily is wearing checkered-flannel sleep pants and a t-shirt. Her long hair is loose around her shoulders.

"You left her in the car?" Aunt Sarah asks the question with the same tone Mom uses when I'm about to be grounded. Even though I'm not on the receiving end, I cringe at the look in her eye.

"The car was locked. I didn't know if it was safe to come in!" He puts his hands up, like he's surrendering in a shoot-out.

Aunt Sarah's face softens. "Of course. I'm sorry." While Aunt Sarah stands in the entryway, the deputies crowd onto the landing by the window.

"Stan, is that you?" Deputy Pelton bounces down the stairs and greets Stan with a slap on the shoulder. "Glad you're here, man. Dave is upstairs."

Stan shakes the deputy's hand, then turns towards his daughter. "Emily, this is Eric, I mean, Deputy Pelton, from my men's Bible study group."

Emily shakes his hand. Her hair falls around her face as she leans forward, and she does a little hair-flip thing to toss it behind her shoulder. "Nice to meet you," she murmurs. She spots me beside the eagle and gives me a weak smile.

Deputy Pelton motions for me to follow Stan and Emily as the group tromps back upstairs. His partner stands at the top of the stairs, hands behind his back and feet spread shoulder-width apart, guarding the muddy footprints.

"What is this, Mrs. Hooper?" Deputy Pelton studies the heavy frame that fell off the wall. He yanks a pair of blue latex gloves from his pocket and pulls them on with a snap. He holds the frame by the edges with his palms, fingers splayed. "Is this valuable?"

Aunt Sarah shrugs. "It's just an old map of the property."

Deputy Chavez speaks up. "It's dated 1927. Is that when the house was built?"

Aunt Sarah shakes her head, "No, the house was built about ten years before that." She points to a spot in the corner of the framed piece. "This is the original boundary line." Her finger trails along the glass. "I don't own this section of land, the vineyard. It was sold in the 1980's."

Deputy Pelton scratches his head. "Has the map always hung in this spot?"

Aunt Sarah tips her head to the side. "I haven't changed things much since I moved in. It looks like it's been there for quite some time."

Deputy Pelton rubs his hands along the back of his neck. "And nothing else is missing or disturbed?"

"Well, the jug with the green stripes. Maybe it rolled under... I don't know." Aunt Sarah shakes her head. "I'm sorry for wasting your time. I just... with the children here..."

"You did the right thing!" Deputy Pelton lifts his eyes to Aunt Sarah. "You shouldn't hesitate to call us!"

"He's right, ma'am," Deputy Chavez says with a grin. "We appreciate the call. Gives us something to do besides eat donuts." His smile fades and his eyes turn serious. "Anytime your home is broken into, you should report it." He looks at our little group and adds, "You were lucky tonight. I think the intruder was interrupted or scared off by something."

"Chester." I bend over to rub the cat's head. "I think Chester scared him off."

Deputy Chavez shrugs. "I guess guardian angels come in all sizes and shapes, huh?"

After the deputies leave, we all stand in a clump in the entryway. Aunt Sarah sighs and rests her forehead against the closed door. I rub my arms, wishing I could scrub away the layer of uneasiness that hovers over us.

"Come on, troops." Aunt Sarah raises her arm straight above her head like she's holding a flag. "To the war room."

We exchange puzzled looks and follow her into the room with the piano. The rug is still rolled into a tube and the furniture shoved against the wall from our dance party. *Was that only a few hours ago? It feels like years.*

"Stan, did you bring your guitar?" Aunt Sarah walks to the piano and rustles through some pages of sheet music.

His smile flashes across the room. "I always have a guitar with me. Hold on, I'll be right back."

"Boys, find a seat. We're going to change the atmosphere in this place."

We exchange more puzzled looks and Alex helps me drag the sofa into the center of the room. Emily and Trey scoot a couple of wing-backed chairs into place beside the sofa. I'm not sure what's happening, but I grab afghans from the room where Aunt Sarah keeps her TV and pass them out. Alex takes one of the wing-backed chairs and Emily sinks into the other one. Trey, Kyle and I settle into the sofa with a crocheted blanket around our shoulders. Chester jumps onto the spot between me and Trey and pushes the afghan around with his giant black paws. When he has the blanket scrunched just right, he snuggles down, paws tucked under his chest.

Stan returns with a guitar case in one hand and a dining room chair in his other hand. He places the chair beside the piano and shrugs out of his leather jacket. He lays the case at his feet and pulls a guitar into his lap. He plucks a few strings while Aunt Sarah plays a single note on the piano. Satisfied at the sound, Stan gives Aunt Sarah a nod. Aunt Sarah closes her eyes and lets her fingers run across the keys. The room fills with sound. Already, I feel better.

"This is from Psalms 3." Her voice is clear and confident as she sings the ancient words. "I will not fear ten thousand that have set themselves against me. I will not fear ten thousand that have circled round about."

About the third time through the song, the rest of us join in. I don't know all the words, but I sing the parts that repeat. I imagine King David singing this, and I feel a tiny bit braver as I think about the boy who faced a giant and later became a king.

A few moments of silence hang in the room and then Stan strums a couple of chords on the guitar. "This one is from Psalm 42. I learned it in the King James version, so the words are old fashioned, but don't let that throw you. God is the same yesterday, today, and forever."

Stan closes his eyes and takes a breath. I expect another gentle song about God's love and protection. Instead, an explosion of sound surges through the room. Stan's fingers move up and down the neck of the guitar. He plays each note with such power that I imagine ancient armies marching to war. His well-defined biceps flex and I study the tattoos on his forearms. *This is not your ordinary worship pastor.*

"Why art thou cast down, O my soul? Why are you disquieted in me?" His voice is deep and gravelly. Prickles run down my spine.

The song thunders across the room and it seems like the lights just got a little brighter. I glance at the chandelier hanging overhead and smile when I see Alex doing the same thing. *He noticed it too.*

"Hope thou in God for I will praise Him again. Hope thou in God."

The old-fashioned words don't seem weird. Instead, I feel each word penetrate deep into my gut. *Hope thou in God. Hope thou in God.*

Stan's voice reverberates through the room. "He has delivered me from my enemy who was too strong for me. In the nighttime His song shall be with me."

I don't know the song but I kind of recognize some of the words from the Bible.

His voice reaches a crescendo and he belts out, "Bless His holy name! Bless His holy name!"

The hair on my arms stands up as though there's electricity in the atmosphere and it feels like the ceiling rolls back for a direct connection to heaven. The fear that has been hovering over me is gone. I feel calm. Brave.

Stan's voice falls silent, but he continues to strum his guitar like a call to battle.

After a few minutes, Aunt Sarah plays a melody on the piano, and Stan strums harmonizing chords on his guitar. Even though no one sings, the music washes over me, and I realize I'm humming along. I don't know how long we sit in the museum-turned-war-room, but when the music finally fades and I open my eyes, I'm as relaxed as a wet noodle.

It takes all my effort to crawl up the stairs. When I slip into the bed – alone this time, the words of the song whisper through my thoughts like a lullaby from heaven. *Hope thou in God. He has delivered me from my strong enemy. Bless His holy name.*

<u>Chapter 6</u>

I wake to the smell of bacon. Glancing around the sun-drenched room, I pull myself into a sitting position. Hardwood floors, a fuzzy white rug, a dresser and a nightstand with a lamp that looks like something from an old western movie. The window has a pull-down shade and one of those swoops of white material looped over the top and down the sides.

The water stain on the ceiling catches my attention. Yesterday, I thought it looked like a map of Idaho. This morning, it looks more like Texas. The rain last night probably has something to do with that.

The grumbling from my stomach is so loud I can't ignore it any longer. With a sigh, I manage to drag myself out of bed. I pad down the hallway to the bathroom and take care of morning business. Grinning at myself in the mirror, I run a hand over the brown stubble that covers my head. *No time wasted on unruly hair.*

When I open the bathroom door, Kyle has his fist raised, ready to knock. "Oh, hey." He rubs sleepy eyes with the back of his hand. "Bacon. Save me some." He shoves past me and slams the bathroom door.

I feel my lip lift in a snarl but stop the snarky comment before it slips out. Instead, I say, "Sure. See you in a minute." *How's that for mature?* Maybe I'll even save him some bacon.

The broken window is now covered with a piece of cardboard and strips of duct tape. The two squatty jugs are back in place on the little carved table. But there's a rectangle of brighter-blue wallpaper highlighting the spot where the framed map should be.

"What's the deal with that map?" I ask the question out loud.

"I've been wondering the same thing." At the sound of Trey's voice, I whirl to see him standing behind me.

So many questions and absolutely no answers. I need food. I follow the scent of bacon to the kitchen with Trey on my heels. Aunt Sarah is sitting at the table with a cup of coffee, and Emily is flipping pancakes at the stove, her long hair pulled into a ponytail that swings as she moves. Stan, wearing a toolbelt and sturdy brown work boots, is fiddling with the door.

Aunt Sarah must have seen my puzzled frown, because she says, "Stan is installing new, more secure locks on all the doors. He was at the hardware store first thing this morning."

I devour four pancakes and a heap of bacon before Kyle straggles in and plops himself into the chair next to me. "I thought I told you to save me some bacon."

"Kyle, that look you gave Brandon could curdle milk." Aunt Sarah winks at Kyle and motions to Emily, who pulls a plate of crisp-fried bacon from the oven. "There's plenty for everyone, no need to be surly."

"Sorry," Kyle mumbles as he grabs a handful of bacon. He shoots me an apology with his eyes. Instead of answering, I shove the last bite of pancake into my mouth and push my chair away from the table.

"I'll help with dishes," Alex volunteers. He's standing in the doorway trying to look nonchalant, but I see him eyeing Emily.

"Seriously?" Trey snorts in his milk. "Do you even know how to wash a plate?"

Alex thumps Trey on the back of the head. "Knock it off, squirt."

Trey jumps from his chair and Kyle moves a protective arm around his plate as he shovels in another bite of bacon.

"Boys." Aunt Sarah's voice snaps us to attention. She gives each of us a laser-glare that sends a shiver down my spine. "Alex, thank you for the offer to help with dishes.

Very generous of you considering I don't have a dishwasher." She motions to the sink and Alex slinks across the room, meek as a puppy. "Kyle, when you've finished your breakfast, you're on dish-drying duty. You'll find a clean dish towel in the drawer to the left of the sink."

"Trey and Brandon, I have a project for you outside."

We follow Aunt Sarah outside. I have to hustle to keep up with her long strides. She's wearing a long, flowy skirt with a pattern of flowers and a t-shirt that seems a little too big for her. She tucks the shirt into the waist of her skirt as we walk, and the clunky beaded bracelet hanging off her wrist gets caught in the material. "Oh, bother."

She stops to untangle the bracelet and I bump into her. Trey stops short, his shoes plowing into the dirt. Aunt Sarah untangles her bracelet and sets off across the lawn once more. We trot behind, still wondering where we're going and what our assignment is going to be. *At least it's not dish-duty. I hate washing dishes.*

"Um, Aunt Sarah? There's a spot on the ceiling above my bed. Yesterday, it looked like Idaho. This morning, it's more like Texas. I think you have a leak."

Aunt Sarah looks towards the house. "From Idaho to Texas, huh? That doesn't sound good." She stares at the roof for a moment, then sighs and turns her attention back to us.

"Boys, take a look at this." Aunt Sarah squats with her skirt brushing against the grass. She points to a tangle of grass and wide, green leaves in front of a picket fence that might have been painted white a long, long time ago. "This is supposed to be a flower bed."

Kneeling beside her, Trey surveys the ground. "Not many flowers, are there?"

"Not that you'd notice, anyway." Aunt Sarah presses her fingers into the soil and scoops up a brownish-white lump. "This is an iris bulb. Do you see it?"

Joining them on the ground, I peer at the bulb. "Yeah, I see it."

She scrapes more dirt off another lump in the ground. "And this is a different kind of flower bulb." Yanking a clump of grass from the flower bed, she sighs. "It's so overgrown that the flowers have a hard time blooming. They need a little more space between the bulbs." She turns to me with a hopeful expression. "If you're willing, I could use a little help. Pulling the grass and thinning the bulbs."

Trey reaches a hand towards the sad, wobbly fence. "You could use a lot of help, I think."

Instead of being offended, Aunt Sarah laughs so hard she snorts. "You are not wrong, Trey. I could use a lot of help."

Still giggling, Aunt Sarah stands to her feet and reaches a hand to me. I let her pull me to my feet. "You're under no obligation but here's my offer. I'll pay you boys ten dollars each to clear the grass from this flower bed. And, if you're interested, we could add painting this poor, dilapidated fence for another ... ten dollars for each of you."

"What about Kyle?" I didn't hear a payment offer for dish duty.

"Oh, yes." Aunt Sarah nods. "The offer includes Kyle. What do you think?"

Twenty bucks? Each? What's to think about?

"Sounds good to me. I'm in." I blurt out my answer before I even consider asking Trey or Kyle what they think. Trey is still staring at the flower bed. "Don't you want to do it, Trey?"

"Talk it over," Aunt Sarah shrugs. "My feelings won't be hurt if you decide not to take on the project. But it *would* be a huge blessing." With a swoosh of her too-big skirt and the clickity jangle of her bracelets, she heads back to the house.

"What's wrong with you? Don't you want to earn twenty bucks?"

Trey stares after Aunt Sarah. "It's not that. It doesn't feel right to take her money. I mean, maybe we should just do this to help. You know, like she said, be a blessing."

"Oh." *And I'm supposed to be the more-mature big brother.*

We're heading back to the house as Kyle bolts out the kitchen door. When he sees us, he barrels across the grass, and I dive out of the way just in time. Kyle springs through the air and tackles Trey with a flying leap. They roll around on the grass, grunting and throwing fake punches as I stare at the peeling gray paint, the off-kilter shutters, and the questionable shingles of the old house. Just as I decide Trey's right about the whole blessing thing, he hooks my leg with his arm, and I hit the grass with a thud. It's wet from the rain last night, and cold.

By the time I'm sitting on top of Kyle with his arms pinned to the ground, we're all breathing hard. Panting, I turn to Trey. "You're right, little bro. Yes, to the flower bed project. No to the money."

"What are you talking about?" Kyle squirms under me, and I let loose of his arms.

Rolling onto the muddy grass, I sprawl out with my arms above my head. I'm still a little out of breath. "Aunt Sarah…has a flower bed…that needs some…work."

Trey, bending over and holding his knees, seems to have recovered a little faster. "She offered to pay us to pull the weeds and thin the bulbs. Oh, and to paint the fence."

"Like Tom Sawyer." Kyle giggles. "Who can we trick into painting it for us?"

"But that's just it," Trey plops down onto the grass. "I *want* to do it. But not for money. I want to *bless* her." He shrugs. "Maybe that sounds lame, but she *could* use some help around here."

Kyle sits up, and the frown on his face tells me he's mulling over Trey's words. "She's got Stan. And Emily. And the orchard workers. They help her."

"Yeah, but look at this place, Kyle."

Kyle stares at the old house, and when he turns back to Trey, he has a huge grin on his mud-streaked face. "Let's get started."

Chapter 7

Aunt Sarah sets us up with trowels, an ancient wheelbarrow to put weeds and grass in, a bucket for salvaged flower bulbs, and a hose. The hose is to be used to soften the ground and rinse tools, but I have some other ideas, too. Like an epic, all-out water battle.

"When the grass and weeds are cleared out so we can actually see the fence, I'll find some paint and brushes." Aunt Sarah wipes her hands across her skirt and then brushes them against each other. "I'll let you get to it, then." As she turns away, she adds, "Who knows? You could have this done by lunchtime!"

Kyle grabs a trowel and shoves it into the compacted soil at the exact same time Trey shoves his trowel into the mud about a foot away. The result? I get a face-full of flower bed dirt. Time for that *other* use for the hose.

After a little bit of hollering, and a lot of messing around, we're ready to try again. Our shirts are soaked, clinging to our spines, but they won't stay wet for long in the pounding Colorado sunshine.

Kyle presses the trowel into the hose-drenched soil. I stand back, wary of more flying dirt. Trey shoves his garden trowel into the ground and pries up a lumpy bulb. I decide to move a little further down. The grass is up to my knees, and there's some kind of weed holding it prisoner against the aging pickets.

"Wouldn't it be cool if we found buried treasure?" Trey jabs the trowel into the dirt and frees another iris bulb, then leans back on his haunches and studies the roofline of the old mansion. "I mean, this seems like that kind of house."

Kyle stabs the ground with his trowel. "That would explain why the guy wanted the map, I guess."

Rubbing dirt-crusted fingers across the back of my neck, I take a deep breath. "Speaking of that…" The image of the map, and the broken window in the upstairs hallway causes a shudder, even though the air is oven-hot. "*Was* he after the map? Why did he go to all the trouble to break into the house, and then not take the map with him?"

"I think Chester surprised him." Kyle yanks on a handful of grass. "Maybe Chester jumped on him and that's how the window broke." He throws the green clump into the wheelbarrow. "The window breaking made a lot of noise. The guy knew we were right there, and he needed to get out fast."

"Maybe, yeah." I don't like thinking about any of this. The slimy feeling washes over me again, and I rub my arms.

Trey stretches out on the ground beside the trench he's cleared. "Do you think Suburban Guy is the one who wants that map?"

"Definitely. I saw Break-in Guy get into the Suburban." I toss a clump of grass on top of Kyle's contribution in the wheelbarrow. "But what I want to know is…why does he want it?"

Kyle lays his trowel down and plops onto the ground beside Trey. "Those guys were scary. Whatever they want, it's not good."

We work in silence for a while. I don't want to think about the intruder standing outside our bedroom door. But I can't seem to think about anything else, and I wonder if Kyle and Trey are thinking about it too.

A shadow falls across the ground. When I look up, Aunt Sarah is smiling down at me. "Looks like you're making good progress."

"No way are we going to be finished by lunch, though."

"Speaking of lunch, it's time to eat." Aunt Sarah takes a couple of steps the other direction and leans over Trey's work area "I've got a few things to do around the orchard after lunch. I'm afraid it might be a little dull for you boys.

Would you like to come with me? Or you can stay here. You're free to roam the property as long as you're careful."

"Yeah!"

"Really?"

"Cool!"

Aunt Sarah laughs. "Was that yes to exploring the property?" She ruffles Trey's hair. "Or yes to coming with me on dull orchard errands?"

I answer for all of us. "Yes, to exploring. Thanks, Aunt Sarah."

"Yeah, thanks." Trey stands and brushes the dirt from his backside. "You're the best."

"Stay near the house, though. Don't cross any fence lines."

Kyle lifts his hand in a Boy Scout pledge. "We promise."

Does that pledge still apply if you're not a Boy Scout?

"That's settled, then. Now, to lunch!"

Chester is waiting for us on the front porch.

Kyle drops to his knees and asks the cat, "Hey buddy, whatcha been doing, huh? Did you miss us?" He scratches Chester behind the ears and is rewarded with a deep, rumbling purr. "You did miss us, didn't you?" Kyle scoops Chester into his arms and staggers a little as he stands up.

I hold the door open for Kyle and Chester and exchange a smirk with Trey as he follows them inside. Who knew

Kyle would be such a softie for a cat? But then, Chester *is* a pretty cool cat.

The air is heavy with spices, and my stomach rumbles as I follow the scent into the kitchen. Four places are set at the table: complete with woven placemats, plates, bowls, napkins, silverware and glasses. Only four? Where's Alex? And Emily? I see a crockpot on the counter and when I lift the lid, a puff of steam fills the air with a savory aroma of meat and vegetables.

"What is that?" Trey's eyes are bright with anticipation. "It smells good."

"Some kind of stew, I think." I peer into the pot and sniff. "With green chilis?"

Aunt Sarah walks to the sink and turns on the faucet. "Emily made some stew for us the other night. I asked her to put the leftovers in the crockpot before she left for work." She squirts a blob of soap into her hand. "Wash your hands, and then we'll see what you think of her cooking."

Kyle turns his nose up at the chopped fresh cilantro that Aunt Sarah pulls from the refrigerator, but I add some to my bowl, along with a squirt of fresh lime juice. I devour the blend of tomatoes, carrots, green chilies, black beans, corn and beef.

"This is good," I manage to mumble in between mouthfuls.

Aunt Sarah just smiles and shoves a plate of cornbread towards me. "After lunch, you boys are free to roam. I'll have my cell phone. Kyle, you've got my number?"

"Uh huh." Kyle nods and shoves a final spoonful into his mouth. He tips the bowl and scrapes the sides with his spoon.

Aunt Sarah pushes back from the table. "Some areas don't have good cell reception." She waves a hand above her head. "I think the mountains get in the way." With a shrug she adds, "But, usually a text will get through even if a call is dropped. We'll meet back here at six o'clock for dinner. The house key is on the rack in the pantry." She scoops the remains of the stew into a plastic container. "Since Kyle did breakfast dishes, Brandon and Trey, you're on dish duty for lunch." She hands Trey a sponge. "If you work together, it won't take long."

With a heavy sigh I haul the dishes to the sink and turn on the hot water. *Whoever heard of a house without a dishwasher?*

As the bubbles form a mound in the sink, I think about calling Mom. Does she know about the break in last night? Probably. Aunt Sarah would have called Mom and told her about it. *Right?*

I turn off the water with a sigh. Closing my eyes, I imagine Mom's voice saying everything's fine, and not to worry. My eyes pop open. *But what if she doesn't say that? Will she make us come home?* I attack a plate with the sponge and scrub as if I can make my worries disappear as easily as a clump of uneaten food. *Besides, I'm not a little kid anymore. I can go a day without my Mom.*

Chapter 8

Finally, I slide the last freshly dried bowl into the cupboard and then try to look at the kitchen like Mom would. The crockpot is not plugged into the outlet. I mark a pretend list in the air with my finger. "Check." The inside part of the crockpot is washed and sitting upside down in the sink. "Check." The rest of the dishes are washed, dried and put away in the cupboards. "Check." I swipe a few crumbs off the table with the dishrag and toss it into the sink. "Done. Let's go."

We bolt from the house and across the lawn. Chester meows from behind the screen door. Kyle runs back and opens the door. "C'mon buddy." Chester strolls onto the porch, blinking in the sunlight. "Um, guys? Should we lock the doors?"

"Do we have the key so we can get back in? Aunt Sarah said something about a key in the pantry." Trey walks back to the house. "I don't even know where the pantry is."

We rummage for a few minutes before Trey discovers not only the pantry, but the rack of keys hanging behind the pantry door. There are about a dozen keys hanging on the metal rack, and none of them are labeled, so we try them all until we find one that fits the lock on the kitchen door.

With the key tucked in his pocket and the cat following on his heels, Kyle rattles the handle of the kitchen door. "Yep. We're good to go."

As the memories of last night darken my thoughts, the excitement of exploring fizzles like a dud sparkler on the fourth of July. "Maybe we should just stay in the house."

"Are you kidding?" Trey stares at me. "Aunt Sarah said it was fine. So. Where do we go first?" Trey turns in a circle as he surveys the possibilities.

I point to the side of the house. "Chester seems to think we should go that way." Only the tip of his black tail is visible as he slips through a bush.

"Then east it is, Chester." Trey races after the cat.

Kyle and I follow, squeezing into the space between the branches. I wince as a twig scrapes my cheek. *Maybe following a cat isn't the best plan.* We tumble into a field of waist high grass and old pieces of wood; crates or pallets that have been stacked and long forgotten. The ground raises up on three sides, with the house behind us.

I can see the Bookcliffs in the distance, but the gently sloping hills block the view of anything closer. "This is cool. It's like a secret hideout."

Kyle climbs to the top of a teetering pile. "Look at me! I'm king of the hill." He raises his hands above his head in triumph.

"Not for long." Trey scrambles after him and knocks Kyle to the ground. I can't see them in the swaying grass, but I can hear the grunts and giggles as they wrestle and kick.

Chester rubs against my legs, and I bend to pet his sleek back. "They're kinda rowdy, huh?" Chester chirrs in agreement. I plop onto the ground beside him, and he bumps his head against my hand. Chester gives a soft meow and moves just beyond my reach. I lean towards him, but he inches a little further away. "Come on, Chester. I thought you liked to be scratched behind the ears." I scoot towards the cat. He takes another step backwards with a teasing glint in his green eyes.

I sit up straight and take a closer look at the pile of junk behind the cat. It looks like the edge of a door. "That's weird." I crawl on my hands and knees until I can touch the edge of the doorframe. "Definitely weird. This feels like it's attached to the hillside."

Chester tilts his head and meows. He stands on his hind legs then presses his paw against the doorframe. I pull wood and weeds away until the outline of a door is clearly visible. The rounded top of the solid wood door is at my eye level. It looks old. And made for short people. I stand on my tip toes and dig my fingers into the dirt around the top, but it doesn't budge. Running my hands along the side, I feel for a space, something to grip. A clump of grass tumbles to the ground, revealing a black metal bar that looks just like the handle on the carriage house doors.

"Guys! Come here!" My voice echoes across the grassy basin. "Come see what Chester found."

The chest-high grass sways as Trey and Kyle make their way towards me. I call out again, so they can follow my voice. "Over here! Hurry!"

"Whoa." Trey studies the strange scene. "Cool."

Kyle climbs the mound above the door and surveys the hillside from that vantage point. "It's a door in the middle of nowhere."

Trey runs his fingers along the edge, like I had a few minutes earlier. "Is it really a door, though? Not just… you know, leaning against the side of the hill so long it got stuck?"

"Only one way to find out." I take a deep breath and wrap both hands around the metal bar. I pull. Hard. Nothing. I try again, and this time, I feel the door quiver beneath my hands.

"It moved!" Kyle's eyes are wide. "Try again, Brandon."

I breath in and out a couple of times and then with all the strength I have, I yank the handle. My shoulders burn with the strain and then… I'm sitting on the ground staring into a black cavern.

"I am *not* going in there." Trey backs away from the opening. "Spiders. Rats. Who knows what's in there? Uh-uh. No thank you."

"Are you kidding?" Kyle rolls his eyes and throws his hands in the air. "You're going to let the possibility of a spider keep you from exploring the coolest thing ever?"

I rub the back of my neck as I consider what might be lurking in the darkness. "Maybe we should at least get a flashlight."

Kyle leans into the entrance and scans the interior. "I've got a flashlight on my phone. Hang on." He pulls it from the pocket of his jeans and then shines a thin beam of light across the entrance. "Yeah, okay. An actual flashlight might be a good idea."

We race back to the house but clump together in the kitchen. None of us has any idea which direction to move.

"Which way should we go?" Kyle asks as he wanders around the kitchen. "Where would Aunt Sarah keep a flashlight?"

Trey shrugs. "Under the kitchen sink? In the carriage house? In the pantry?" Trey opens the cupboard under the sink as I start towards the carriage house.

"Got it!" Kyle comes out of the pantry with a yellow and black flashlight, the kind with a handle. It's heavy enough he's holding it with both hands.

He takes off across the lawn at a gallop with the giant flashlight clutched against his chest. Trey trudges behind with his hands in his pockets and his head down.

"Oh, come on." I bump Trey with my hip as I walk beside him. "It's going to be cool."

This time, I'm careful to keep the branches away from my face as we slip through the bush and emerge into the field. Even though I know where the hidden doorway is, I can't see it until we pass the pile of old wood. Chester waits in front of the open door, smoothing a paw over his whiskers.

"I get to hold the light since I'm the one who found it." Kyle hugs the yellow and black plastic against his chest like I'm going to fight him for it.

"Whatever. Just turn it on." I roll my eyes and motion for him to go first. He hesitates as the beam of light flickers across the sloping dirt path. "Go!" I nudge him across the threshold. "Trey? Are you coming?"

"I'll stay here," Trey says. "You know, as lookout."

"Okay. If that's what you want to do." Hunching over a little to get through the door, I blink a couple of times to let my eyes adjust to the gloom. Putting my hand against the wall as the ground slopes downward, I feel tree roots pressing through the hard-packed dirt. Chester darts between my legs and I let out a little-girl squeal as he scurries ahead.

"Brandon? Are you okay?" Trey's voice already sounds far away.

"I'm fine!" My toes slide inside my too-big high-tops as I take cautious steps through the darkness. "Kyle, slow down. I can't see." I pause, listening. "Kyle?"

My heart is pounding in my ears and the blackness seems to press around me, making it hard to breathe. The ground is uneven. Careful and slow, I step forward. And just like that, my foot slips, my ankle twists and I go down. Hard. I can't breathe. Something hard is poking my hip. I can't see a thing. *This isn't nearly as fun as I thought it was going to be.*

I hear a noise up ahead. Scratching. Rustling. My skin prickles and I try to force away the image of a pack of hungry rats. *I'm sitting right at rat-chewing level.* My heart is pounding in my ears and panic swells through my chest.

A memory verse that I learned in Sunday school runs through my mind, and I whisper it out loud. "God has not given me a spirit of fear, but of power, love and a sound mind." I feel the panic ease a little, so I say it again, louder. "God has not given me a spirit of fear, but of power, love and a sound mind." The same prickly feeling that I had when Stan was singing washes over me, and I can hear the guitar in my mind. I feel calmer. I don't exactly feel courageous, but the fear has ebbed away, even though I still can't see a thing in the inky blackness.

I move the rock from under me. Only it's not a rock. It's square, and the sharp edge has left a sore spot. "Kyle! Stop messing around. Where are you?" As I stand, a shooting pain races from my ankle to my knee. "Agh." I press against the wall and take a limping step forward. Two glowing orbs appear ahead of me, and I gulp. *Is it a rat?*

"Mer-ow?" The green orbs disappear and appear again as the cat blinks his eyes.

Not a rat. I exhale a shuddering breath of relief. "Hey buddy. I'm glad to see you."

"WAA! Ha ha ha." Kyle leaps from behind the curved wall of the passage with the flashlight under his chin. Kyle's face glows a creepy red in the beam of light.

"Kyle! You jerk."

"Scary, huh?"

"Stop messing around." I point to my ankle. "Thanks to you, I tripped on something."

"Guys?" Trey's voice floats through the passage. "What's happening in there?"

"Brandon's hurt." Kyle's shouted reply echoes back.

"What should I do?" Trey sounds shaky and scared. "Is it bad? Kyle? Do you have your phone?"

Kyle flits the beam of light across the rounded top of the tunnel and then sweeps it across my face. I squint my eyes against the blinding white light.

"I'm okay." I holler back. "Kyle, stop with the flashlight. Go get Trey."

Rubbing my aching ankle, I blink a couple of times, but all I see is a lightshow of colorful spots. Chester meows softly to let me know he hasn't abandoned me. "Thanks, buddy." I scratch his fuzzy head. "Maybe we should let *you* carry the flashlight from now on."

My eyes are finally spot free when the golden beam of light bounces over the rough dirt floor as Kyle and Trey make their way towards us. When they round the corner, the light glints across a square object.

"Hold up, guys." I point towards the square. "Kyle, shine the light over here." I bend over and stare at the box. "I have a bruise from that, whatever it is." I run my fingers over the ridges of intricate carving along the sides. "What a weird place to leave a jewelry box."

Kyle holds the light a little higher and we crowd together in the amber glow as I try to open the box. I feel along the edges and tip it all directions, but I can't find a top or bottom.

"Can we… maybe… check it out in better light?" Trey glances over his shoulder with a hopeful expression.

"My ankle is feeling better." I put a little weight on my foot and try not to wince. "Aren't you curious to know where this tunnel ends up? I don't think it's much farther."

"Here, Brandon." Kyle hands over the flashlight. "I'm sorry. I didn't mean for you to get hurt."

"I know." Reaching for the flashlight, I pause. It's heavy. He's been using two hands to carry it, and I want one hand free to brace myself against the wall. "You can carry it, Kyle. Trey, why don't you carry the box?"

We set out again, slower and a little more cautious this time; Kyle in front, Trey clutching the wooden box as he stumbles behind the beam of light, and me in the back so no one can see my limp. My shoe is feeling tight, and every step sends a jarring zing of pain from my ankle to my kneecap.

We follow a curve to the right, then a curve to the left. The ground continues to slope down. The ceiling is so low that we walk hunched over, like chimpanzees. Kyle dances the light across a wall of bricks.

"This is the end."

"It can't be the end. There's nothing here." Trey clutches the wooden box a little tighter against his chest. "There has to be a way out." I can hear the panic in his voice.

I can also just make out a faint melody. "Kyle, is that you?"

"Is what me?" Kyle gives me the raised eyebrows.

"Listen. Do you hear music?"

Peering into the shadowy corners, we listen. To absolute silence.

"I don't hear anything." Kyle shrugs.

Trey shakes his head. "Me neither. But it's creepy in here. Shouldn't we turn around?"

Chester sits beside Trey and licks a paw. He doesn't look concerned at all as he swipes the wet paw across his whiskers. "Mer-row." The cat stretches and yawns and then walks to the wall of bricks. He stands on his hind legs and meows again. His white-tipped paw flicks against a thin string hanging from a brick that's a different color than the others.

"What's he saying?" Trey looks as though he expects Kyle to interpret cat-language.

"There's a string. It looks like it's hanging from a brick." Kyle hands Trey the flashlight. "Shine it right here." Kyle bends over the odd-colored brick. "Good boy, Chester! Guys, check it out!" Kyle picks at the edge of the brick. It comes loose in his hand, and now we see a metal ring.

"Now what?" Trey asks in a shaky voice.

"Kyle, pull it!" I smile encouragingly. "You've got this."

Kyle takes a deep breath and wraps both hands around the metal ring. He plants his feet in the dirt and pulls. The brick wall slides across the ground, leaving an arc pattern in the dirt. Trey steps away from the just-opened gap with wide eyes.

Kyle is still holding the ring with both hands when I poke my head into the opening. I can't believe my eyes.

Chapter 9

Alex is sitting on a bed, the last note he played on his guitar filling the room with a sound like a strangled buffalo. His eyes are enormous, and his mouth reminds me of the clown that hovers over the last hole at the mini-golf place.

Alex leaps from the bed and turns in a circle. "What? How?"

Kyle and Trey tumble into the room after me. Chester slips between our legs and hops onto the bed beside the guitar. He snuggles into the blanket and tilts his head, like he's also interested to hear our story. We all start talking at once, blurting out bits and pieces.

"We followed Chester into a field-"

"But then we came back to get a flashlight-"

"Chester showed us the brick that covered the doorknob-"

"There was a door in the field and Brandon opened it-"

"We found a jewelry box in the tunnel-"

I slump to the floor, unable to stand on my swelling ankle any longer.

"Oh, and Brandon hurt his ankle." Kyle finished the story with a shrug and pointed the flashlight at me.

Alex turns and his expression changes from surprise to concern. He kneels beside me and tugs my jeans up to get a better look. He peels down my sock and lets out a low whistle.

"Kyle, turn off the flashlight. Or at least stop shining it in my eyes." I wince when Alex prods the side of my swollen, grapefruit sized ankle.

"Dude." Alex lifts his eyes to mine and I can tell that he's worried. "How long ago did this happen?"

"Just a couple of minutes ago." I pull my pantleg back down to cover the blotchy red skin peeking out from my sock. "It's fine."

"That is not fine." He runs his hands through his hair and walks back and forth across the tiny space between the bed and the gaping cavern behind the just-opened doorway. Alex stares into the tunnel. "And discovering a secret entrance to my room is kinda freaking me out." He stands in the entrance to the tunnel and peers down the corridor. "Let's close this back up. For now."

"Uh, how are we gonna do that? There's no handle on this side of the door." Trey scratches his ear and glances into the darkness beyond the bedroom. "I can push from the other side, but then I'll be in the tunnel. Again."

Alex pulls on the door, but it doesn't budge. With a sigh, Trey tugs Kyle through the doorway. "We'll be right back. Grab the flashlight, Kyle." Together, Kyle and Trey shove against the door, and it closes with a loud snap. A faint crack in the wood paneling is all that shows of the doorway.

"He's right. There's no way to open it from this side." Alex rubs his hands across the smooth surface where a doorknob should be located. "Freaky."

"Yeah, I wouldn't want to sleep in this bedroom." Glancing around the room, I take in the exposed brick on the opposite wall. "Is it a bedroom?"

"I think it used to be a storage room. Or maybe a wine cellar. Aunt Sarah loaded up all the junk that was down here and turned it into a guest room." Alex runs his hands through his hair again, leaving a spikey ridge on the top of his head. "I remember seeing some barrels of stuff in front of this wood paneling. That kinda makes sense now. To block off the entrance."

Leaning against the wall, I close my eyes and try not to think about the weird, achy tingle running from my ankle to my knee. I'm doing some deep breathing I learned in Judo class when Trey races back into the room holding the giant flashlight. "It was easier going through the tunnel this time."

Kyle stomps down the stairs behind him. "Because you had the light."

"You could have used the flashlight on your cell phone."

Alex puts his hand up and glares. "Enough about the flashlight. Trey, get some ice for Brandon's ankle."

Trey runs up the stairs and then his footsteps thunder overhead.

Alex plops beside Chester onto the bed and pulls his cell phone from the guitar case. A moment later, I hear Mom's voice. For some stupid reason, I have to blink away a couple of tears. *I'm not crying. I'm not.*

"I'm not sure what to do. Yeah, it's swollen. Red. Trey's getting ice, but we don't have it on the ankle yet. I don't know. You can ask him. He's right here." Alex shoves the phone into my hand.

"Hey Mom." I try to keep my voice light, cheerful. *No problems here. I am not crying.*

"Hey yourself." Mom's voice comes over the phone. "Brandon, I want you to explain how your ankle feels. Does it hurt to put weight on it?"

"Yeah, a little bit."

"Are you bleeding? Are you dizzy? What happened? Details, mister."

"I stepped in a hole and my ankle twisted. I guess I landed wrong or something." *I totally hate being fussed over – and I do not want to screw up the Cousin Crew time by a dumb old injury.* "Um, it only hurts when I stand on it. The rest of the time it's just kind of…throbbing. It's no big deal, Mom."

"Okay." She sounds calm and that makes me feel better. But I can tell she thinks it might actually be a big deal, and that's kind of reassuring too. "You're going to need some x-rays. Let me talk to Alex again."

Alex holds the phone tucked under his chin while listening to Mom. "Stan dropped me off on his way to join Aunt Sarah. I'm not sure where they were going." Alex pokes my ankle and asks, "Does that hurt?" I shake my head and try not to make whimpering noises. "He says no, but his face is the color of chalk and he's chewing his lip, so I don't believe him." Alex runs his hand through his hair again while listening to Mom's reply.

Trey clomps down the stairs with a bag of frozen corn. I take it from him, noticing the smudges of dirty fingerprints we're both leaving on the plastic bag. I plop the veggies across my ankle with a shudder. The weight of it is more uncomfortable than the cold.

"Did you tell Mom about the secret door?" Trey grabs for the phone. "Don't hang up yet! Mom! We found a secret door in the field behind the house and a tunnel that leads to Alex's room in the basement."

Mom's voice carries clear across the room. "What?"

Trey goes through the whole story for Mom, leaving out the part where he didn't want to join us in the tunnel, and ending with us tumbling into Alex's room. "Brandon fell in the tunnel." Trey listens for a minute and then hands me the phone. "She wants to talk to you again."

I wipe my damp palm down my jeans, leaving a muddy stripe, before I take the phone. "Mom?" My heart rate speeds up. *Just how much trouble am I in now?*

"Brandon, you found the secret entrance?"

"Well, umm… yeah. Chester found it. We just followed the cat. Wait. You knew there was a secret entrance?"

"Uncle Joe used to tell Aunt Bekki and I stories about a secret entrance. There was a map of the property on the wall upstairs. It had some strange markings on it, but we never could figure out what they meant. We never knew if the secret entrance was real, or something Uncle Joe made up."

"It's real. It's awesome." I glance at the paneling in Alex's wall that opens into the tunnel. "And a little creepy."

"Wow. That's quite a discovery. But I need you to promise that you'll stay out of the tunnel until Aunt Sarah knows about it."

I rub my throbbing ankle and nod my head. "I promise."

"Good." I hear her take a deep breath. "Alex is going to take you to Grand Junction for x-rays. Call me when you get the results."

"Okay, and Mom? I'm sorry."

"Accidents happen." Her voice is soft and makes me feel like crying again. "I'm sorry I'm not there to take care of you. I love you, Brandon."

"Bye, Mom. Love you too." I hit the button to disconnect and hand the phone to Alex. Wiping my eyes with the back of my hand, I hope nobody notices the tears.

"Okay, squirt. Let's get you up the stairs." Alex grabs my shoulders and hoists me into a standing position. I cringe at the pain that races up my leg and limp my way to the stairs. Alex is in full-commander mode as he barks out orders.

"Kyle, write a note for Aunt Sarah and let her know we're taking Aunt Bekki's Chevy to get Brandon checked out at the emergency room."

"Or I could just text her." Kyle answers with a little snark in his voice.

Kyle shoots off a text while I hobble to the carriage house and plop into the passenger seat. "Did I call shotgun? Because I'm *so* riding shotgun." I tip my head against the headrest and close my eyes. An angry rhythm pounds with each heartbeat from my foot to my knee.

"You've got it, little bro."

Now I know Alex is worried. He's being nice.

Chapter 10

I don't even open my eyes when Trey and Kyle jump into the backseat and slam their doors. With Alex behind the wheel, Aunt Bekki's brand-new Chevy is racing across smooth black top before I muster the strength to peek at our surroundings. The streets of Grand Junction whiz past, and then I see the brick tower of the hospital on our left. Alex pulls into the emergency area and hops around the front of the car to help me out. He leaves the engine running as we walk up the ramp like we're practicing for a three-legged-race.

Four hours later, I walk back down the ramp with a clunky plastic boot to support my officially-broken ankle. The shot they gave me makes my head feel like a balloon and my stomach is threatening to do terrible things. Aunt Sarah walks behind us with the phone pressed against her ear. She met us at the hospital and has been on the phone with Mom just about constantly.

"No, they made an appointment with an orthopedic specialist for Friday. Until then, he's in a boot." Aunt Sarah listens for a minute, and then with gentleness in her voice, answers Mom. "Of course. We'll see you in the morning. What's that? Oh, yes. I'll tell him." She drops the phone into her purse and taps my shoulder. "Your mother says she loves you. She'll see you in the morning. And call her later tonight."

Alex has the car waiting in the same spot, and Kyle and Trey are in the backseat, noses pressed against the windows like a couple of Labradors. Alex opens the passenger door and waits for me to position myself in the bucket seat. He buckles the seatbelt around my waist like I'm a little kid. I'm too tired to complain.

"Aunt Sarah will fill the prescriptions on her way home." Alex studies me out of the corner of his eye as he waits at the red light. "Will you be okay for an hour without the pain medicine?"

"I'm fine." *All this fussing makes me feel like a dork.*

"You don't look fine," Kyle pipes up from the backseat. "Your face is a funny color."

"That's because I'm about to hurl. Other than that, I'm fine."

"Okay. Whatever." Kyle sniffs and turns his face towards the window. He wipes his nose with the back of his hand. *Is he crying?*

"We're going to stop at the burger place on our way home." Alex glances at me. "What do you want?"

What do I want? To *not* have slipped and fallen in a dark tunnel. To *not* have a throbbing, broken ankle. To *not* smell stinky onion rings and French fries all the way back to Palisade while trying *not* to barf all over my aunt's new car. Ugh. "How about a strawberry shake?"

Alex orders a boatload of stuff from a drive-through and hands me my shake. The car fills with the aroma of fast food and my stomach lurches angrily. I swallow hard. *No, no, no. Not in Aunt Bek's car!* Holding the cool paper cup against my forehead, I press the button to roll the window down. I gulp in the fresh air and let the wind whip across my face for a few minutes. *Better.* By the time we pull into Aunt Sarah's curved drive, I'm slurping the last bits of strawberry through the straw.

I manage to get out of the car and stumble to the front porch with the crutches under my armpits, and the clunky plastic boot leaving a weird pattern in the gravel. Aunt Sarah must have the pharmacy on speed dial, or she drove that antique car of hers awful fast, because she got home before we did. She meets me at the door and the worry in her bright blue eyes says more than any words she might have spoken. She gets me settled on a worn leather couch in the TV room, fusses with pillows under my foot, and brings me ice water in a glass with a straw. Thankfully, Alex ordered more than just a strawberry shake for me because now I'm starving.

While I wolf down a cheeseburger and fries, Trey and Kyle go through the story again for Aunt Sarah. Aunt Sarah sits quietly, her attention flitting from Trey to Kyle as they tell the story about our afternoon. It sounds a little crazy even to me, and I was there.

Trey ends the tale with an enormous shrug. "So, that's what we were doing when Brandon fell. The tunnel is dark and has a steep slope in that part. I think he tripped on the little treasure box."

"I stepped in a hole."

"Oh. Yeah, that makes more sense. It's not a very big box." Trey's eyes go wide. "Where *is* the jewelry box?"

Kyle jumps to his feet. "It's still in Alex's room! I'll get it." He turns to Aunt Sarah. "Maybe you can figure out how to open it."

"My mom said something that I wanted to tell you about, Aunt Sarah." I lick salt from my fingertips and swallow the last bite of fries. "That map upstairs, you know, in the frame?" Aunt Sarah nods and her eyes flicker with interest. "Mom said that Uncle Joe showed her and Aunt Bekki the map when they were kids. He told them about a secret passage. The map had some clues, but they never found anything. Mom thought it was something he made up to entertain them."

While I was talking, Alex had grabbed the map from its spot in the hallway. I wiggle into a sitting position and swing my legs onto the floor. Before I can stand up, Aunt Sarah plops into the middle spot on the couch and pats the cushion on the other side, indicating that Alex should sit there. Alex lays the framed map across her lap.

Aunt Sarah squints at the map. "Let's see if we can decipher this." She puts on a pair of glasses hanging from a chain around her neck. "I wish Joe had told me about the secret passage and mysterious hidden doorways. I had no idea."

"Maybe he didn't know either," Alex says as he settles into the cushion beside Aunt Sarah. "That creepy doorway in the room downstairs is practically invisible when it's closed. I haven't been to the field, but if Chester hadn't helped them out, I don't think the boys would have found that door."

Kyle comes back into the room with the wooden box clutched to his chest. Chester marches in behind him and rubs against my plastic boot. I try to pick him up, but he's too heavy. The cat stretches his paws towards me and with a chirring sound, he hops into my lap.

"But how could Chester know about the secret passage?" I rub under his chin, and he rewards me with a loud purr. "The doors were closed on both ends of the tunnel."

"Maybe there's another way into the tunnel, like a cat-sized entrance." Kyle plunks onto the floor by my feet and scratches Chester behind the ears. "I'll bet there's little spaces that cats and mice and stuff can fit through. He probably goes in there to hunt for mice."

I shudder at the memory of the scratching sounds in the tunnel. "Yeah, maybe."

"What about this?" Trey takes the little chest from Kyle and studies it. "This is a weird jewelry box. It doesn't even have a lid or a latch."

"Could I see that?" Aunt Sarah reaches an age-spotted hand towards Trey, and he hands her the chest. She turns it over and then holds it up to the light. "It's a puzzle box."

Trey stands behind the couch and peers over her shoulder. "Can you open it?"

"I'm not sure." Aunt Sarah tips the box and runs a finger along the side. "I know it takes a specific series of moves to open, but I'm not good with puzzles."

The doorbell rings. Alex puts a hand on Aunt Sarah's shoulder. "I'll get it." He stifles a yawn as he walks out of the room.

Seeing his yawn triggers one of my own. My ankle hurts and even though I'm really interested in the puzzle box, I'm tired. With a firm push, I roll Chester off my lap.

He settles beside me and closes his eyes. I wish I could do the same.

"Hey, Brandon. Sounds like you had a little excitement this afternoon." Emily and Stan follow Alex into the room. Emily holds out a white paper bag. "We picked up your prescriptions."

"Thanks." Taking the bag, I fight back another yawn. "You know anything about puzzle boxes? Or maps?"

"Puzzle boxes? Maps?" Emily lifts her eyebrows and shrugs. "No, sorry, I don't know much about either."

"I found a YouTube video. Here Aunt Sarah, check this out." Kyle shoves his laptop towards Aunt Sarah. She adjusts her glasses and peers at the screen. Everyone crowds around Kyle's computer. Except me.

I slouch against the leather cushion and glare at my throbbing foot. Opening the white paper bag, I study the bottles inside. Liquid Ibuprofen. Mom gave me that when I had a fever. *Liquid is for little kids, but not choking down a pill would be nice, too.* I dig out the last bottle and read the label. Tramadol. It has a bright orange warning label across the top. *Yikes.* I drop it back into the bag. Which one do I take? *I wish Mom was here.* Oh, I was supposed to call her! *Did we call Mom?* As if she has radar, Alex's phone rings.

"Oh shoot! It's Mom!" He presses the phone to his ear. "Hey Mom. I was just about to call you."

Yeah, right.

"She wants to talk to you." Alex shoves the phone in my face and whispers, "We were just about to call her." I glare at him and take the phone.

"Hey, Mom." My voice cracks. I bite my lip. *Stay tough, Brandon.*

"Brandon, how are you?"

"Oh, you know, broken ankle. But I'm okay." *Liar, liar, pants on fire.* I glance at my pants as if they might spontaneously combust. "I'm supposed to see a specialist on Friday."

"Well, we're praying for a good report on Friday." She sighs. "I'll come get you tomorrow."

"What about the Girl Scouts? As soon as the group you've got now leaves on Saturday, the next group will be checking in."

"The Girls Scouts can do without me for a day." She pauses and I can picture her looking up as she makes a plan. "I can get Roberta from the restaurant to cater for us tomorrow."

Suddenly, I realize that as much as I'm missing Mom, I want to be here. With Kyle, Trey, Aunt Sarah, and Chester. And even Alex. I want to know what's in the puzzle box. And why Suburban Guy wants that map.

"Brandon? Are you there?"

"Yeah, Mom, I can hear you." I take a deep breath. "This isn't exactly the way I imagined our visit with Aunt Sarah going, and I miss you, but… I'd rather stay here." I glance at Aunt Sarah and her blue eyes sparkle. "If it's okay with Aunt Sarah, I mean."

The fan of fine lines crinkle down Aunt Sarah's cheeks as a smile lights her face. "If you feel up to it, I'd like for you to stay. Tell your mom I'll call her back in a bit."

"She says I can stay." I feel a goofy smile on my own face as I add, "She'll call you back in a bit."

"You're sure? If you change your mind, just say the word."

"I'm sure. Thanks Mom."

"Well, then. You should get to bed and put that ankle up, okay? I'll see you on Friday. And take it easy."

"I will." At this moment, I mean it, too.

"Good night, Brandon. I love you."

"Love you, too." The phone goes quiet, and I hand the phone back to Alex. Heat creeps up my cheeks as I realize everyone is staring at me. "What?"

"Glad you're staying, that's all." Alex rubs his hand across my bristly head and a crooked smile flits across his face. "You're pretty tough, little bro."

"That may be, but it's time for Brandon to call it a night." Aunt Sarah takes the bag of medicine from me and, adjusting her glasses, she studies the labels. "Let's get you to bed. Are you able to get up the stairs?" She frowns at the plastic boot and the crutches laying in front of the couch.

Alex and Kyle heave me off the couch and I head towards the stairs with the crutches under my arms. It's not pretty, but I make it up the stairs and to my room. Staring at the boot, I wonder what to do next. After wiggling around like a demented caterpillar, I'm eventually settled in the bed with clean teeth, a clean t-shirt and basketball shorts, and Chester snuggled against my leg.

Aunt Sarah gives me one of the tablets from the bottle with the scary orange label and leaves ice water on the bedside table. She stands for a moment at the bedroom door but doesn't say anything before slipping back downstairs. I stare at the Texas-shaped spot on the ceiling as the voices from downstairs fill the house. The bed is soft and warm, and the dull ache in my ankle relents as the white pill does its thing. I rub Chester's silky ear and let his purr lull me to sleep.

Chapter 11

"You'll find pancakes and bacon on the table. The rest of us have already eaten but I didn't want to wake you. Trey and Kyle are coming with me this morning. I have a meeting and then I'm going to take that old map to a friend of mine. Big Jim knows a lot about old things, and he might be able to shed some light on what's so special about that map.

"Alex is helping Stan install new flooring at the guest houses today." With a twinkle in her eyes she adds, "Unfortunately for Alex, Emily is working all day."

"Yeah, too bad for Alex." I can't help the smirk. Nobody will be around to appreciate how cool Alex thinks he looks in a toolbelt.

"Will you be alright by yourself?"

"Sure. I'll be fine." *I think.*

She frowns as if she doesn't believe me. "I can skip the meeting."

"It's okay. Really. I'll call Alex if I need something."

"I suppose he will be nearby." She turns her gaze towards the spot on the ceiling. "That really does look like Texas."

"What time is it, anyway?" I grab the crutches from the foot of the bed and position them under my arms.

"Ten o'clock. Like I said, I didn't want to wake you." She smiles as Chester reappears in the doorway. "But Chester is a different story. He runs a tight ship."

Wow. Mom would never let me sleep this late. She and Chester would get along great.

I wave from the kitchen door as Aunt Sarah, Kyle and Trey roar off in the old Land Rover. As soon as they disappear around the bend in the trees, I plop three pancakes on a plate and pop it in the microwave. I crunch a piece of bacon while I watch the turntable spin. The microwave dings to let me know my pancakes are ready. Yanking my hand back from the too-hot plate, I hope I haven't turned them into concrete. It's weird to be in someone else's house all by myself.

I chomp my bacon and pancakes in silence, then wash the dishes and put them in the wire rack next to the sink. A note on the counter, written in Aunt Sarah's spidery scrawl, almost gets obliterated by my too-wet sponge as I wipe crumbs from the counter. It takes me a couple of tries before I decipher what she's written. *Stan's number, her cell number, leftover pizza in the fridge.* The landline phone is beside the paper, and I pick it up as the grandfather clock in the hallway chimes the half-hour. I look around the freshly wiped counters and drip-drying dishes and feel a surge of pride. *Responsible and tidy. That's me.*

I clomp past the grandfather clock with its slow tick-tick-tick echoing through the hallway. Stretching out on the brown leather couch in the TV room, I plop the phone onto the floor, within easy reach. *Now what?* I should have found the remote before I sat down. Heaving myself onto my elbows, I scan the tabletops for the remote.

The puzzle box catches my eye. Did Kyle find the right YouTube video? Did they get it open? I pick it up and turn it over. I don't think it's been opened, but someone took the time to clean it up so that the patterns and colors in the wood gleam in the sunlight.

I can't find the remote and I can't figure out how to turn on Aunt Sarah's TV. Kyle's laptop is sitting on the low wooden table, and I spend way too long trying to figure out his password before snapping the screen shut with a groan. It's obvious that I am *not* the technology whiz in the family.

A shelf on the wall beside the window, filled with books and games, seems like my only entertainment option. I pull the curtain open to let in more light as I sort through the dusty game boxes. *Scrabble.* No. *Clue.* No. *Yahtzee.* No. *500-piece jigsaw puzzle.* Ugh, boring, but maybe.

With a sigh, I scan the book titles. The books themselves are bound in leather and appear to have been read many times. *Ulysses* by James Joyce. No. *Little Women*. Absolutely no. *The Mysterious Affair at Styles* by Agatha Christie. Probably not. Rubbing my hands across my head, I try to scrub away the frustration.

Then, I spot something that might actually be worth reading. The books surrounding it are leather-bound and have fancy lettering. But this book has a faded cloth binding, frayed around the edges. Blowing a fine layer of dust from the greenish-gray cover, I lift it from the shelf. *Puzzles and Puzzle Boxes.* The publication date on the first page says 1925. *Whoa. How long has it been sitting on this shelf?*

I thumb through the brittle pages and my heart skips a beat as I turn to a yellowed page with a drawing of a box that looks a lot like the one in my lap.

Settling onto the couch with the book and the wooden box, I prop my feet on a couple of throw pillows. I concentrate on the detailed set of pictures and the old-fashioned typeface that explains how to "open the mysteries of the Far East." According to the book, this box has somewhere between ten and fifteen-hundred combinations of movements to get it open. *Great.* And if I force it, I'll break it, and it will never open. *Even better.*

Chewing my lip, I study the mosaic pattern on the top of the box. It doesn't look like the fifteen-hundred-moves kind of box. I read through the numbered pictures again and jiggle a section of the box, then twist, turn and twist. The top of the box slides open, revealing a wad of red velvety cloth in the center of the box. My hand shakes as I feel something heavy wrapped in the folds of cloth. An old-fashioned skeleton-key falls into the palm of my hand. *A key. To what?*

I reach for the pocket on my pants and realize these basketball shorts don't have a pocket. I lay the key on the table and scrutinize the box, then the pictures in the book. *There's got to be more.*

I twist, turn and twist again. A panel on the bottom of the box pops open. A piece of paper, curling around the edges, flutters into my lap. My hand is still shaking as I squint at the scrap of paper. Drawings. Of a flower? Delicate ink strokes form the outline of a blossom. Slanted, old-fashioned letters spell out … what? It's even harder to decipher than Aunt Sarah's handwritten note from this morning.

I set the paper on the table next to the key and stare at the unusual script. It seems familiar for some reason. The map! The bottom of the map has the same handwriting.

I jump from the couch and turn in a circle looking for the map. Where did it go? Maybe Aunt Sarah hung it back up. I clomp up the stairs with my crutches only to find the empty spot on the wall where the map used to hang. Running my fingers across my stubbly head, I take a deep breath. Where could it be? *Oh, shoot.* Aunt Sarah took it with her. The guy in Palisade was going to look at it.

The clock downstairs chimes the half-hour again, and my stomach rumbles in response. Okay, so it's only been an hour since I finished breakfast, but I'm hungry. I head to the kitchen hoping there are a couple of pieces of The Geek left. Or the Supreme. Actually, it was all good.

Chapter 12

With my head in the refrigerator and my booted ankle stuck to the side, I hear a voice outside the kitchen window. Figures. Alex has radar when it comes to food. He and Stan must have come by for lunch. I hope there's enough pizza left for all of us.

My skin prickles as I catch movement out of the corner of my eye and realize it wasn't Alex's voice that I heard. A man is standing on the other side of the kitchen window. The half-open kitchen window! With a whimper, I slide to the floor and sit with my back against the refrigerator. *Who is this guy? Does he see me?* My crutches lean against a chair. *Will he see those and know that I'm here?*

"No, the old lady left a little over an hour ago. There's a grower's meeting today, so she should be away for at least another hour. She had the brats with her."

Not all the brats went with her, buddy.

"Yeah, I'll find it. They all looked the same to me. I grabbed the wrong one, but I won't let you down again, boss."

The knob on the kitchen door rattles and I hear a loud *thunk* as his weight crashes against the door. I don't remember flipping the deadbolt, but I must have, because the man swears and walks away.

As fast as I can, I move towards the front door with my clunky boot, wincing with each step as my weight crashes onto my ankle. The door is locked, but I double check that the deadbolt is securely in place. As I lean against the solid wood, the doorknob moves, twisting back and forth. He's on the other side of the door. *What should I do?*

"Oh Jesus, help me." I whisper a desperate plea for help.

Alex. Call Alex. *Where's the phone?* I fight down the panic and picture the phone lying beside the couch where I had tossed it. Just before I figured out the puzzle box.

The puzzle box! I left it in plain sight on the coffee table, along with the mysterious scrap of paper and the old key. I can't let this guy – this thief – get his hands on those!

I crawl towards the TV room, whisper-praying as I go. "Jesus, help. I'm scared. Show me what to do."

Whispering the Bible verse that's running through my mind, I move across the floor. "God has not given me a spirit of fear, but of power, love and a sound mind." My heart rate slows, and I take a breath. The rest of the memory verse pops into my head and I blurt it out. "Second Timothy 1:7."

Suddenly, my mind is filled with Stan's song from the other night. I can hear his voice as he belted out an ancient prayer that seems like my very own right-now-prayer. I begin to whisper the words into the empty room.

"Why are you cast down O my soul? Why are you disquieted in me?" I snort. "Disquieted. How about freaking out?" But a new thought pops into my head.

Say no to fear. Say yes to God's way: power, love, sound mind.

The song flows over me as I take a long, slow breath and concentrate on the words.

"He has delivered me from my enemy who was too strong for me."

"Jesus, deliver me from this enemy."

I grab the phone and close my eyes, trying to remember Alex's number. His number shows up in Aunt Sarah's contact list. "Thank you, God," I whisper as the phone dials.

Alex answers on the first ring. "Hey bro, what's up?"

"Uh, there's a guy trying to break into Aunt Sarah's house." I try to keep my voice from cracking. "I was in the kitchen, and he was outside the window talking on his phone. He saw Aunt Sarah leave with Kyle and Trey and thought the house was empty."

I can hear the panic in Alex's voice. "Where are you right now?"

"TV room, on the floor." The words of my prayer circle over me. *He has delivered me from an enemy too strong for me.* "Alex, what should I do?"

"Stan and I are on the way." I hear muffled voices and then he says, "I'm calling 911. Don't move."

"Yep." I stare at the phone for a second, wishing that lifeline with the voice on the other end hadn't fallen silent. I let out a huge sigh, and the slip of blue paper quivers in the stream of my exhaled breath. Whatever this guy is after, I can at least make it hard for him to find my recent discovery. I slide the scrap of paper into the *Puzzles and Puzzle Boxes* book and grab the old-fashioned key. With the book in one hand and the key in the other, I crawl across the room towards the bookshelf. I plunge the book back into the empty slot on the shelf and stare at the heavy metal key. I slide it into the box with the picture of horses and shove it into place. A quick swipe across the top of the box erases my dusty fingerprints. My back presses against the shelf as I pant like a marathon runner.

I'm over-reacting. The guy is probably long gone by now.

Glancing at the window beside the bookshelf, I swallow a scream at the sight of a face peering through the window. He has his hands on either side of his eyes, but I don't think he's seen me. Yet. I close my eyes and wish I could turn myself invisible.

Power. Love. Sound mind.

The glass in the window beside me shatters with a loud crash and the man is halfway through the window before I open my eyes. I'm not sure which of us is more startled as our eyes meet. He struggles into a standing position and with a wild surge of adrenaline, I leap to my feet. Crouched. Ready for battle.

Mom's Judo instructions come flooding back into my memory. *Move fast. Be bold. Low center of gravity.*

Before he has a chance to react, I surge into motion. Right hand, collar. Left hand, elbow. Awkward boot behind his knee. Step in fast. Clip his thigh. Hard. And he's down! On the ground. *Whoa. That actually worked.*

I follow him to the ground. While he fights for the air that I've just knocked from his lungs, I scan my opponent. He's on the scrawny side, thankfully.

Before he's able to pull in a breath, I throw all my weight onto his chest. Pin his arms beneath my knees. With my arm across his throat, I pant into his acne-scarred face.

"Who are you?" All I get in answer to my question is a wide-eyed stare. His mouth makes little fish-like gulps, but he doesn't speak. *Oh. I didn't mean to put him in a strangle-hold.*

Moving my arm away from his throat, I sit upright, knees locked against his wrists. He jerks his hips, trying to dislodge me. *Nope. Not gonna happen.*

Just as I'm about to pound my fist into the guy's face, Alex comes barreling through the room. "Brandon! Whoa." Alex slides across the wood floor, curling the rug into a lump as he reaches me. "What is happening? Who is this guy?"

"He… the window…" I lower my raised fist and allow Alex to pull me to my feet.

He has delivered me from my enemy who was too strong for me!

The words circle in the air above me as glass crunches under my feet. The man is covered with tiny cuts and a feel a brief stab of pity for him. Until I remember that he just broke a window and crawled through it.

Alex stares at the man lying on the ground. "I called 911. The sheriff's department is on the way."

Stan steps towards the man on the ground and places a boot on his chest. "You stay put, amigo. You're not moving a muscle until the cops get here. Understand?" Stan's tattooed forearms twitch in readiness.

"Are you okay? Brandon?"

It takes a second before I realize Stan's talking to me.

"I'm good." *Breathe in. Breathe out.* "Yeah." Closing my eyes, I feel a calmness that doesn't make any sense considering the guy laying on the floor. And my ankle doesn't even hurt. The words of my prayer bounce around in my thoughts as I open my eyes. *Hope in God. Bless His holy name!*

Feeling like my bones are turning to liquid, I look around for my crutches. Which I left in the kitchen.

As if he's reading my mind, Alex gives me a scolding big-brother look. "Where are your crutches?"

"Kitchen." Cringing away from his disapproving glare, I add, "I was kinda busy. Hiding. From the guy."

"It looked to me like you were pounding him to a pulp."

I kind of was, wasn't I?

He has delivered me from my enemy who was too strong for me. Bless His holy name!

The words of the Psalm still swirl above me, but Alex's criticism crowds the room. Another crunch of glass under my boot fills me with frustration and the gentle, whispering praise vanishes like a puff of smoke.

"That was impressive, Brandon." Stan's grin brightens the room, and my defense-response eases. "But get off your feet now, okay?" He motions to the couch.

My legs are a little rubbery. Alex hovers behind me, watching each step. *I might not be looking as tough as I'd like.* As I sink onto the couch, the doorbell rings.

Alex scurries away and returns a moment later with Deputy Chavez. My stomach growls. I know it's ridiculous, but all I can think about right now is the pizza sitting on the kitchen counter. Thankfully, Deputy Chavez seems more interested in putting the intruder in hand cuffs and getting him into the backseat of the patrol car.

Just as I'm about to suggest we pop the leftover pizza in the oven, Deputy Pelton walks in. I sigh and swing my leg onto the pile of cushions. I'm so hungry. *Do we have to do this now?*

Officer Pelton squats beside me and says, "You sure do know how to keep things interesting, huh, buddy?"

The last bits of calm and peace that had wrapped around me evaporate. "I didn't ask this guy to break into Aunt Sarah's house and fall through a window right in front of me!"

"No, I suppose not." He reels backwards a little and his eyes take in my plastic boot and the tower of cushions. "Are you okay?"

"Sure. Other than a crazy man just broke into the house, I broke my ankle yesterday, and I haven't had any lunch, I'm terrific." I close my eyes and take a deep breath. "Sorry. Maybe I *am* a little stressed."

"I'll try to be quick, okay?" He looks at Alex and Stan. "I'll get your statements in a minute." He turns his attention back to me. "Tell me what happened, Brandon."

"I was in the kitchen, getting the pizza out of the refrigerator when I heard the guy outside. He was on the phone."

"Do you know who he was talking to?"

"He called the other person Boss."

"Okay." Deputy Pelton wrote on his little form. "Then what?"

"The kitchen door was locked. He slammed against it, but it didn't open. I ran to the front door to make sure it was locked. He rattled that door too." I take a shaky breath. "Then I remembered that the phone was in this room, so I crawled in here to get the phone."

"Okay. You crawled to the phone."

I nod. "Yeah, and I called Alex. And he called you."

"Why didn't *you* call 911?"

With a shrug I admit, "I don't know. Alex was the first person I thought of." He nods for me to continue. "So, I'm by the window with my eyes closed and he crashes through. And then, I used an *osoto gari* and took him down."

"Excuse me?" Deputy Pelton pauses his scribbling and gives me a puzzled look.

"It's a Judo throw."

"Oh, right. Judo. Brandon, I'd say there's more to you than meets the eye." He smiles and shakes his head. "Now, how about you find some of that pizza while I write up an official statement for you to look over?"

He pulls me to my feet, and I grin back at him, relief flooding over me. "Yes, sir. That would be great."

Chapter 13

Deputy Pelton waves from the window of the squad car as he drives away. The guy in the backseat doesn't look up. *Is he embarrassed at being tackled by a kid?* The smug grin on my face is wiped away by the memory of crawling through the house in a panic. I whisper the words that had changed everything. "God has not given us a spirit of fear, but of power, love and a sound mind."

No matter how much I'd like to pretend my judo moves are awesome, I know the truth. It wasn't until I talked to Jesus that things turned around.

Alex gives me a weird look but doesn't say anything. Maybe he thinks I'm losing it. But everything is crystal clear to me. *I prayed. Jesus answered.*

I wolf down two slices of cold ham and pineapple before anyone else decides they're hungry. The last slice is stuck to the bag by a glob of cheese. As I wiggle my thumb under the congealed mass of cheese, Aunt Sarah, Kyle and Trey slam through the kitchen door like a hurricane.

"We saw the cops driving away. There was a guy in the backseat!" Trey plops down beside me and I swat his hand away from the last slice of pizza with a growl. Maybe I'm still a *little* hangry.

"Yeah, it's been … uh …" Alex sends a help-me look towards Stan. Stan returns the look with a shrug.

"We were only gone a couple of hours." Aunt Sarah's forehead crinkles. "There were orchard workers nearby. I…oh." She sinks into a kitchen chair, grips my hands in hers and stares at me with those intense blue eyes. "Brandon, are you alright?"

"I'm okay. Honest." I avoid Aunt Sarah's laser-like gaze and feel the all-too-familiar flush creeping up my cheeks as I shove the last slice of pizza towards Trey. "Here, Trey. I'm not hungry anymore."

"Well, now I *am* concerned." Aunt Sarah's teasing tone catches me by surprise, and I feel my mouth twitch in the beginning of a smile. "Did you at least save some room for a cinnamon roll from Slice O' Life Bakery?" She places a white paper bag on the table, opens it with one hand and wafts the fragrance towards me with the other. "We brought a few home." Aunt Sarah places a hand over her mouth and the concerned frown crinkles her forehead again. "Oh, my goodness. Has everyone eaten?"

"Alex and I have sandwiches at the job site." Stan steps towards me and puts a hand on my shoulder. "We'll get back to work on the guest cottages *after* Brandon tells you what you missed." He adds a wink when I roll my eyes.

I grab a cinnamon roll from the bag. It's huge. Gooey. And smells like heaven. Tearing off a piece of fresh-baked wonder, I go over the details of the morning again, but this time, I add the part about the scripture-song-prayer and my divine help and add the part about opening the puzzle box.

The cinnamon roll disappeared while I was talking, and now my hands are sticky. I start to wipe them on my pants and come into contact with my bare leg poking out from under the basketball shorts. Without a word, Aunt Sarah hands me a damp cloth from the sink and I wipe the frosting from my fingers.

"There are drawings of flowers on the paper in the puzzle box. I couldn't read the words, but the writing reminded me of the bottom of the map."

"Really?" Aunt Sarah's eyes glitter with interest. "Kyle, we left the map in the Land Rover. Could you bring it in?"

"Yeah. Be right back!" Kyle races to retrieve the map, with Trey following on his heels. Done with the washcloth, I totter to the sink and toss it across the faucet. Then I slug down a glass of tap water while we wait for Kyle and Trey to return. Aunt Sarah pours herself a glass of water and sits at the table. Kyle barrels through the kitchen door with the frame under his arm and Trey trailing behind.

"Whoa! Slow down, Kyle." Alex glares at the boys, in commander-mode once again. "You too, Trey. We've had enough broken glass around here for one day."

"Sorry." Kyle places the framed map on the kitchen table and he and Trey scoot into chairs. They wiggle back and forth in the chairs as the anticipation builds. *Treasure maps and mysterious puzzle boxes will do that to a guy.* Even me, I realize as I tip the chair back onto all four legs.

"That reminds me," Stan says. "Alex, we need to run into town and pick up a couple of replacement windows. We'll get them in before nightfall."

"Right." Aunt Sarah rubs a hand through her tornado of white hair. "We'll feel more secure with those in place before dark. Thank you." She dismisses her helpers with a two-fingered wave.

Chapter 14

Kyle, Trey, Aunt Sarah, and I circle around the kitchen table. We have the puzzle box, the key, the little piece of paper with curled edges, and the framed map all laid out in a row. Aunt Sarah positions her glasses on her nose and picks up a round magnifying glass with a light built into the handle.

"Brandon was right," Aunt Sarah says, peering at the map. "The writing across the bottom matches the puzzle-box paper."

"What does it say?" My elbows hit the table as the chair slams onto all four legs. I didn't realize I had been tipping it. Again.

Aunt Sarah jumps and places her hand over her heart. "Brandon! Stop tipping the chair." She turns back to the blue paper and aims the magnifier-light next to her crooked finger. "Here's a blossom. The letters beside it spell out

Tunnel A." She moves her finger. "Now a picture of two blossoms and the words Tunnel B." She slides her finger across the page again. "Tunnel C. Three blossoms."

She pulls the map closer and points at the miniscule peach blossom markings. "One blossom marks the first tunnel, two blossoms for the second tunnel, and three blossoms mark the third tunnel." She looks at me over the top of her glasses. "Well done, Brandon. You recognized the handwriting on this blue paper. It's the same as the signature and date right here." She taps her finger against the glass that covers the bottom edge of the map.

Her praise washes over me with a hot rush, and my chest swells with pride for a split second. Until it hits me. "Three tunnels?"

Aunt Sarah hands me the magnifying glass. "See for yourself."

Turning my attention to the map, I trace the blossom-lines with my finger. One. Two. Three. ABC.

Trey gives me a wide-eyed stare. "The map shows three tunnels?" The smattering of freckles stands out against his pale cheeks.

"Yeah." I point to the line on the map that corresponds to the one-blossom marking. "See? It goes from behind the house and into the wall right here. Into the bedroom downstairs."

"So, Chester found Tunnel A. But there are two more?" Kyle shakes his head. "Whoa."

Aunt Sarah's eyebrows are so high they've almost disappeared as she stares at the map. "Look at this. Behind the fireplace in the mausoleum – I mean, music room!"

Kyle and Trey take turns staring at the map as I bounce in my chair. *This is wild!*

Leave it to Trey to bring the excitement level down a notch with a valid question. "If you're right about the tunnels, this is only two. Where's the third one?"

Kyle snatches the magnifier from Trey. "I see it. Here." He traces a line with his finger. "But it's not even close to the house. Both ends of that would be outside."

"An outside only tunnel." Trey sighs. "That's a good thing. I think."

"Do you remember the night you arrived?" Aunt Sarah stands to her feet and paces across the kitchen. "Alex was out in the storm because Oscar was in the orchard."

"Oh, right. I remember Oscar. The neighbor's horse." Kyle lays the magnifying glass on the table. "You have leads and halters in the carriage house because the neighbor's horses are here so often." Kyle pushes his chair away from the table. "Are you thinking what I'm thinking?"

"It's possible, isn't it?" Aunt Sarah's eyes are shining.

"What?" Trey looks from one face to another, and I can tell he thinks we've lost our minds. "What are you talking about?"

"Three tunnels," Aunt Sarah explains. "One leads to the property without using a road, and the other two lead into the house."

"That's totally creepy." Trey shivers. "Why would you want that?"

Aunt Sarah scrunches up her face. "I think it's creepy, too. The man I showed the map to this morning, Jim, said that this house was built during Prohibition." She turns to Trey. "Have you ever heard of Prohibition?"

I'm glad she asked him and not me, because I have no idea.

Trey shakes his head and shrugs his shoulders. "No."

Aunt Sarah takes a sip of water and then explains in a teacher-voice. "During Prohibition, it was illegal for people to manufacture, transport, or sell alcohol, including wine. The law, also known as the Eighteenth Amendment, was in effect from 1920 through 1933."

Aunt Sarah looks at the map and her expression softens. "Honestly, the people who supported Prohibition, or the Temperance Movement, as it was called, had good intentions. But it was a tough law for folks who made their living from vineyards. In fact, many of the vineyards here in Palisade were destroyed by well-meaning enthusiasts of Prohibition."

"Wow. That seems kind of harsh." Trey chews his thumb. "What about this place? Was the orchard destroyed?"

"No, the orchard was left in place. But the vineyards? I don't know. All of those vineyards you saw from the ridge, used to be part of this estate." Aunt Sarah stares out the window for a moment. "This house was built at the beginning of Prohibition." She turns back to our huddle around the table. "I think my husband's family may have been bootleggers. People who smuggled or sold illegal alcohol." She nods as our mouths drop open.

Kyle blurts out, "The grandfather of a missionary was a smuggler?"

Aunt Sarah shrugs. "According to family history, he made a lot of money in the 1920's. Jim verified that this map is hand drawn and was made in 1921. It was signed and dated by the artist." She taps the blue paper. "The same artist who also wrote the puzzle-box note."

"Secret entrances and smuggling would be a hard secret to keep, wouldn't it?" Kyle wrinkles his nose and holds up a finger. "I mean, the workers doing the building would know." Kyle holds up another finger, making a V-sign. "Somebody was buying the secret stuff, right? Palisade is a hard place to keep a secret. I'm sure it was the same a hundred years ago."

Aunt Sarah nods. "Very good points. Our secret tunnels might not be such a secret after all. Other people may know about, or at least suspect, their existence."

"Suburban Guy," Trey whispers. "And Giant-Driver-Guy."

Cringing at the memory of Suburban Guy and his driver, I pat Trey's shoulder. "Yeah, but we don't even know if we're on the right track yet. The Prohibition thing makes sense, but we're just guessing." I pick up my crutches and work for a moment to get them settled under my arms. "Let's see if the fireplace in the music room has any surprises for us."

"Hey, wait a minute." Kyle looks around the room. "Where's Chester?" He glances towards Chester's food and water dishes, in their usual place beside the kitchen door.

"I don't know." A stab of concern shoots through my stomach. "I haven't seen him all morning. Not since he woke me up."

Aunt Sarah nods towards the half-empty dish of cat chow. "He'll come back when he's hungry. Cats are independent. Resourceful." She winks at me as she adds, "A lot like you boys."

The rubber ends of the crutches squeak on the hard floor as we make our way towards the music room. Kyle and I both take a couple of detours as we check places Chester might be cozied up for a nap. Aunt Sarah's probably right, but I can't help feeling a little concerned about our furry friend.

The floral rug has once again been laid across the gleaming marble tiles, and the blue-upholstered furniture arranged in a semi-circle around the room. The tall, narrow windows beside the piano let in enough sunlight that I can see dust particles dancing through the air above the keyboard. Just as we step into the room, the doorbell rings. We all jump at the unexpected sound.

"Oh, blast." Aunt Sarah waves us into the room. "See what you can find. I'll be back in a minute."

Chapter 15

"In the movies, there's always a bookcase." Kyle chews his lip as he scans the room. "You know, move the right book and the secret door opens up."

Trey puts his hands on his hips and glares at Kyle. "Yeah, well in cartoons, the fireplace flips around to reveal a secret room."

"Oh, please. We're not in a cartoon. Or a movie." I roll my eyes and try to remember the markings on the map. "Trey, get the map. That will help."

From the hallway, a barrage of Spanish conversation has gotten so loud that we all pause, wondering what's happening. Peeking around the doorway, I see Aunt Sarah and three of the orchard workers in a huddle. In Spanish, Aunt Sarah gives instructions, and two of the men nod and step back onto the porch.

As Aunt Sarah holds the door open for them, one of the men says, "*Lo siento, Senora.*"

Aunt Sarah gives him a gracious smile and says something that must mean it's okay because he looks relieved as she closes the door.

Now just one man is left in the hallway with Aunt Sarah. The top of his head is even with her shoulder. He twists a dirty ball cap in work-worn hands and nods when he catches sight of me in the doorway. Aunt Sarah says something in Spanish, and his weathered face cracks into a smile. "Nephews, yes." He rubs his hand over his heart and says, "You make Senora happy."

"Boys, as much as I want to stay and help you with, uh, this project, I'm needed at the packing shed." To herself, she mutters, "It's always something. And always expensive."

With a shake of her head, she raises her voice to normal volume. "Stan and Alex will be back before long with the windows, and I have my cell phone. Call me if there is any trouble. And I do mean *any* trouble."

"Yes, ma'am." Trey answers formally. Kyle and I just nod our agreement.

As soon as the front door closes, all thoughts of the orchard and packing sheds evaporate. We walk around the room pressing bricks and wiggling random things, trying to find a hidden lever. Nothing. We study the map and walk through the room again. I slide down the wall in frustration with my back against the mantle. I'm thinking about an ice pack for my grumbling ankle when a faint scratching sound catches my attention.

"Did you guys hear that?" *Scritch. Scratch.* And here I am, smack-dab at rat-chewing level. Again. Ugh! A shiver runs across my neck and down my spine.

"What?" Trey frowns and turns in a circle. "I didn't hear anything."

"Shh! There it is again." Cocking my head to one side I hiss, "Listen."

Trey's eyes go wide. He hears it this time. *Scritch. Scratch. Scratch. Mer-ow.* "It's Chester!" Trey drops to his knees beside me. "Chester! Here kitty, kitty." We hear another faint meow and more scratching noises. "Where is he?"

"I don't know. It sounds like he's in the fireplace." I turn to study the shadowed interior. Soot. A couple of fancy metal things that hold the wood. Nothing else.

"The fireplace is empty. Not even a piece of wood." Trey crawls inside the square space with his butt sticking out of the opening. His voice echoes against the smooth, stone walls. "Chester? Where are you, buddy?"

"Mer-ow." *Scratch. Scratch.*

"Move over." Kyle bumps Trey with his hip and drops to the floor beside me. "Brandon, look at the map. Double blossom. Tunnel B, right?"

"That's what we're looking for, yeah." I squint at the tiny writing. "So?"

Kyle rubs his thumbnail along the interior of the fireplace. "Double blossom. Right here." He rubs a spot on a glossy marble brick and when he pulls his blackened thumb away, I can see what he's talking about.

We push, tug, pry and pound on that brick, but it doesn't budge. Chester is chirring and meowing on the other side, as if he's trying to give us pointers. "I wish I understood cat language."

"Guys?" Trey stands up and I can tell by the gleam in his eye that he's discovered something. Following his line of sight, I let out a low whistle. On the bottom of the mantle, there's an indentation. A keyhole. Trey has the old-fashioned skeleton key in his trembling hand. It takes him a couple of tries to get the key into the space. It takes him a few more tries to turn the key once it's fitted into the hole.

I don't know what I expected. Something more dramatic, though. Instead of the room spinning, or a secret door popping open, all that happens when Trey finally gets the old, metal key in place is that the piece of marble with the double-blossom mark on it pops out of place just enough that I can get my fingers around the edge. Several years-worth of black soot fall all over my clothes. And finally, just when I'm about to give up, the stone tile is in my hand and Chester's green eyes blink at me through the opening.

"Mer-rer-row." Chester saunters into the room with a flick of his tail, leaving black paw prints across the white tiles.

"Anyone want to guess what Chester was saying?" Kyle grins as he wipes his thumb on his pants. "I'm pretty sure he said, 'Took you long enough'."

The opening is only about a foot across. Big enough for a cat, but not for me. Slithering on my stomach into the recess of the fireplace, I stick my arm into the space recently occupied by Chester, and my fingers brush against a metal latch. If I only had a …

Kyle plops down beside me with the flashlight on his phone turned to extra-bright. "Need a light?" He wiggles his eyebrows, and I can't help but laugh. "I promise not to shine it in your eyes this time, and" he crosses his heart with his finger, "No joking around. I swear."

My fingers press against the metal bar, and the stone wiggles. "Move the light a little to the left." Jiggling a little harder this time, the marble piece slides into a grooved slot, revealing a square opening about three-feet wide. I move out of the way so Kyle can shine the light into the cavern.

"What's it like in there?" Trey squats so he can peek over Kyle's shoulder. "Is it like the other tunnel?"

"Huh uh." Kyle crawls forward until I only see the bottoms of his shoes. His voice echoes back to us. "I can see daylight at the other end already."

"Kyle?" Trey crawls into the space. "Kyle, where'd you go?" Trey crouches on his heels then disappears into the darkness just as the doorbell rings.

Pulling my attention from Trey's disappearing shoes, I turn to the empty room. Almost empty. Me and Chester.

"Who could that be?"

Chester chirrs and tilts his head.

"You're right. Bad guys wouldn't ring the doorbell."

Chester leads me towards the front door, leaving a trail of charcoal-colored paw prints across the expensive floral rug. I look down at my soot-covered clothes and wipe my hands across my shorts. I peer through the hole in the front door and collapse against the door in relief. Kyle!

Wait. Kyle? "How did you get out there?" I demand as I swing the door open.

"Well, duh! You watched me." Kyle laughs as he steps into the house. "Trey will be right behind me."

I clomp across the front porch and peer around the side of the house just in time to see Trey scoot out from beneath an evergreen bush. Running my fingers across the soft fuzz on my head, I move towards the bush. With an awkward plop, I kneel in front of the scratchy green branches and spy a cast-iron grate at the bottom of the chimney. Instead of being flush against the house, it swings back and forth on rusty hinges.

Soldier-crawling under the bush, I wiggle into the dark space. A sticky tangle of spider webs hits me across the face. *Is this space filled with black widows? Brown recluse? Are they climbing all over me right now?* I claw at the gummy strands and scream like a little girl.

"Brandon! What's happening? Are you okay?" Trey's shadow blocks the light as he crawls in behind me.

I take a shaky breath and swat away the last of the spider webs. "Sorry. Just…spiders." I slither onto the cool marble tiles of the fireplace.

"Talk about a drama king." Trey shoves me further into the room. "I thought you broke your other ankle or something."

"I just… I don't like spiders." I pull a wad of spider-gunk off my neck. A fresh wave of shivering rolls across my shoulders. "You could have warned me."

"Seriously? It's like eight feet from one end to the other. You were so brave in the first tunnel, and then fighting off the bad guy this morning. I thought a few spiders would be no big deal."

"Yeah." The heat crawls up my neck and burns across my face. *Fear took over. Again. And leaves me looking like an idiot.* "You're right, a few spiders are no big deal." Time to change the subject.

"That's two tunnels." I rub my hand across the back of my neck, trying to wipe away the embarrassment along with the last few strands of spider gunk. "What about the third tunnel?"

Kyle sits down in front of the fireplace with me and Trey. "I think I know." His eyes sparkle with the secret he can't wait to share. "Remember the first day we were here, and Aunt Sarah took us on a tour of the property?"

Trey nods. "Yeah, in the side-by-side."

"Right, and we saw the Jones place." Kyle raises his eyebrows. "Remember?"

Wiping my hand on my shorts, I bob my head in agreement. "We saw the Jones place from the hill, and then she took us to see the guest houses."

"Right. When that map was made, the Jones place was part of this property. A vineyard. Think about it." Kyle's eyes glow. "We saw four horses in the pasture, including Oscar. And then just a few minutes later, Oscar was here. How did he get here before we did?"

Trey uses large hand gestures and speaks slowly, like Kyle might not be too bright. "We stopped at the guest houses."

Jumping to Kyle's defense, I shake a finger in Trey's smug face and notice a spider-web tendril clinging to my thumb. "Yeah, but we were in the ATV's." Using my other hand, I pull the sticky glob off my thumb and wipe it across the floor. "We would have been going faster than a horse, or at least the same speed. And we didn't see any horses on our way." I turn to Kyle. "How *did* Oscar get here before we did?"

"A secret passage."

Trey snorts. "Oh, please. Oscar the horse crawled through a tunnel."

"Not exactly. But maybe..." Kyle leaps to his feet. "Come on, guys. Let's check it out." He leans down and offers me a hand. "And grab the map!"

Chapter 16

I'm not sure who's idea it was to take the side-by-side. But here we are, with Kyle behind the wheel and Trey riding shotgun, the map across his lap. Chester is holding on for dear life in the back seat with me.

Bouncing across the tidy rows of trees, the scent of ripening peaches in my face, I almost forget that we're doing something dumb. Almost. Does Kyle even know how to drive this thing? Potential disasters race through my thoughts for a few seconds before I rein in my imagination and take a deep breath. *God has not given us a spirit of fear, but of power, love, and a sound mind.* This decision might not fall into sound mind category. But, so far, so good, at least.

I lean forward and shout into Kyle's ear. "Shouldn't we check in with Aunt Sarah?"

"She won't mind," he bellows back.

Who left Kyle in charge? I'm four months older, after all. "She said to call!"

Trey shoots a worried glance over his shoulder and when our eyes meet, I know he thinks I'm right. "Give me your phone, Kyle."

"It's in my pocket. I can't reach it right now."

"Kyle, pull over." My voice is demanding, and when Kyle turns to look at me, the side-by-side veers to the right, tilting us onto two wheels. Trey squeaks as Kyle slams on the brakes and the engine stalls.

Trey holds out his hand, palm up. "Your phone. I'm texting Aunt Sarah." His voice is shaky. Mine would be too, if I dared to speak.

"How does this sound? Found second tunnel. Checking out Kyle's theory on third. Took side-by-side. Back soon." Trey holds the screen up so I can read the text. "Do we need to add anything else?"

I squint at the message. "No, that about covers it." Worry tightens my shoulders. This may not have been one of our better ideas. "We should text Alex too."

"Okay." Trey copies the message and I hear the ding as he shoots it off to Alex. "Done."

"Ready?" Kyle turns the key and the engine sputters back to life. Chester sinks his claws into the upholstery as the side-by-side vaults onto the path. Running my hand across his smooth black fur, I whisper a thank you that he's not using my leg for stability this time. I still have the marks from our last ride together.

After a few agonizing minutes, Kyle steers the ATV across a field and pulls to a stop beside the giant cottonwood tree with the heart-shaped branches. We tumble out of the vehicle, taking deep gulps of the sweet, summer air. We stare once again across the valley at the rugged stone cliffs of Mount Garfield, the lush rows of green trees and well-tended grapevines, the brilliant blue sky. Kyle points out the triangle-shaped pasture, the four horses, and the red-tiled roofs of the Jones place.

"When the map was made, this all belonged to Uncle Joe's family." Kyle points at a dark green strip of trees. "The trees grow along the edge of the stream."

Trey chews his thumb as he stares across the valley. "It's pretty. But I don't see anything special." He glances at me and then yanks his thumb out of his mouth and rubs his wet thumb across his pant leg. His flaming-red cheeks contrast with his super-cool tone of voice as he asks, "What's your theory?"

Kyle runs back to the ATV and grabs the map, still in the heavy wood frame. When he reaches the edge of the cliff, he holds the frame at arms' length. "On the map, there's a line across the edge of the pasture. See?"

"Isn't that the fence line?" Sunlight glints across the glass front, making it hard to see the details underneath.

"That's what I thought at first." Kyle squints against the glare and then lays the frame on the ground. "But no other fences are marked on this map." He traces the line with his finger, leaving a smudge on the glass. "This is the outside-only tunnel."

Sinking to my knees beside Kyle, I study the landscape stretched before us. "But it's not a tunnel, is it?"

"Exactly." Kyle's eyes sparkle as he sits beside me. "You see it, don't you?"

"See what?" Trey stares into the distance, trying to figure out where I'm looking. "And I don't think Chester is going to help us with this one."

"He doesn't have to help us this time." Kyle hefts the cat onto his lap. "He led us to the first two, and we figured the last part out ourselves."

"We did?" Trey flops onto his stomach and puts his chin in his hands. "You're gonna have to explain it to me, because I still don't see…" Trey sits up. "Oh! I do see it!" He stands and points across the valley. "It's a little canyon!"

Kyle thumps Trey on the leg. "I knew you'd see it. Eventually." Kyle runs his hand along Chester's back. "It was still Chester that reminded me of it, though."

"How's that?" Trey and I both ask at the same time.

"Brandon, you weren't with us when Aunt Sarah took the map to Big Jim. But he's got a cat that looks like it could be Chester's brother. I was petting the cat while Aunt Sarah was talking, and I saw a painting."

Trey says, "I have no idea what this has to do with anything."

"Be patient. I'm getting there." Kyle rubs Chester's ears and then stares across the valley. "The painting was called Smuggler's Gulch."

"Smuggler's Gulch?" I echo the name back to Kyle. "And let me guess. It's a painting of this canyon."

Kyle wiggles his eyebrows and twirls a pretend mustache. "With one little detail that only a super-investigator like myself would notice. The artist painted the scene from the other side of the canyon." He gives us a second to think about that. "I probably wouldn't have noticed it myself, except for one thing. This cottonwood? It's in the painting." Kyle leans back on his elbows and stares into the spiral of leaves overhead. "I mean, how many trees could there be with branches that twist into a heart shape?"

"That means that Big Jim knows about the secret entrances." Trey stares at the valley below. "Or, one of them anyway."

"Why did Aunt Sarah take the map to him in the first place?" I wonder out loud. "Is he a map specialist?"

"I'm not sure if he knows a lot about maps, exactly," Kyle answers. "He was a history professor. He retired from the university, but he still blogs about local history, and does presentations at schools and stuff. Maybe that's why Aunt Sarah took it to him?"

"I wonder if he likes to paint local history too. Like you said Kyle, the secret entrances might not be a well-kept secret. Maybe Big Jim likes to paint places that have stories that go along with them."

"Maybe." Kyle stands to his feet and brushes the grass from his backside. "I'm ready to find that secret entrance. Who's with me?"

Trey and I leap to our feet. We're *so* ready.

Chapter 17

Kyle bends over the map for another look, then walks in a circle around the giant cottonwood tree. Trey and I sit in the shade of the tree while Kyle stares across the red-stoned valley. He steps towards the edge of the cliff and waves to us. "It's this way! I think."

Dropping to the ground, Kyle scoots to the edge of the cliff and dangles his feet over the edge. He raises his arms above his head.

"Kyle!" My heart stops beating as my cousin disappears over the side of the cliff. Trey and I share a moment of frozen panic before I suck some air into my lungs and crawl to the spot. Peering into the sheer-sided drop off, I brace myself for the worst.

Instead of my cousin's bloody guts, I see an open space on the right side of the rock wall. And then, Kyle appears in the space in the rock. My head drops between my knees, and I take a couple of deep breaths. "Thank you, God.

Whew." When I trust my voice not to crack, I lift my head and motion Trey over. "It's okay. He's not dead."

Trey kneels beside me. "Oh, thank God." He lets out a whoosh of breath. "I thought he was roadkill."

"Guys! Come on!" Kyle waves his arms over his head like he's signaling a landing airplane. "Down here!"

It's not that we don't see him. We're both wondering how to get to there. Even if I wasn't in a plastic boot, I don't think I'd try it.

"Brandon, Trey, you're in the wrong spot. Take a couple of steps to the right. No, I mean the left. My right."

With a confused frown, Trey slides to the left. When his face lights up, I follow his movements. And a silly grin lights up my face, too. Impossible to see unless you're standing directly over them, are three jagged steps carved into the rocky cliff. I clamber down behind Trey and within moments, Trey and I are at the entrance to Smuggler's Gulch.

"Is this awesome or what?" Kyle is bouncing on his toes and high-fives us as we stumble into the canyon.

I see Chester's black and white silhouette at the top of the carved-rock stairs. "Chester? You coming, buddy?" He answers by sticking one hind leg in the air and beginning a serious bath. I guess we're on our own this time.

We scramble over a pile of rocks that must have pinged down the steep cliffs during recent rainstorms. Further into the canyon, I notice rounded rocks and a layer of mud along the center of the path. I've hiked enough mountain trails to recognize a dry creek bed when I see one. This valley is probably filled with muddy water after a storm. Like the one we had the other night. With a nervous glance at the sky, I hope today's weather forecast didn't include rain.

When I look back down, I notice some deep, round-shaped marks in the mud along the canyon wall. Horses! With my hands on my knees, I peer at the tracks in the mud. At least one horse has been through here recently, maybe more. And some deer.

Excited to share my discovery, I look up in time to see Kyle and Trey disappear around the curve in the rock. "Guys, wait up!" My shout bounces back to me, echoing against the sheer cliffs that loom on either side. "Wait up! Up… up…" It's not until I step on a loose rock and my good ankle tilts to the side that I realize I don't have my crutches.

This is about half-way through Smuggler's Gulch, I think. And I really want to see the other side. The tingling pain shooting from my ankle to my knee makes the decision for me. Sliding to the ground, I lean against the rock wall and stretch my legs across the dry, sandy soil that lines the edge of the canyon. I should have looked a little more carefully before plunking myself down, though. I missed landing in a pile of fresh horse manure by about a foot. The stabbing sensation in my leg eases to a grumbly throb, and after a couple of deep breaths, the pain ebbs away.

Cotton ball clouds dance across the ribbon of blue sky above and I have a vague sense that Trey and Kyle should have been back by now. But as I settle into the quietness, my concerns drift away on the breeze brushing against my skin. They can take their time.

The sound of tinkling pebbles bouncing across the dry riverbed registers in my sleepy brain. *I must have dozed off!* Opening my eyes, I find myself staring into a pair of very big, very brown eyes with the longest, thickest eyelashes I've ever seen. A girl. A very little girl. Sitting so close she's almost in my lap.

Shoving against the canyon wall, I try to scoot away. And realize the looming cliff now poking into my spine has me pinned. I study the tiny heart-shaped face and the fringe of shining black hair. The girl's face lights up with a smile that shows a gap on the bottom where she lost her first tooth.

"Hola."

I blink and try to register what's happening. *Oh man. Spanish?* "Hello. I mean, *hola*." I wrack my brain for the few Spanish words I know.

The sparkle in the girl's eyes gives me the feeling that she's amused. "My name is Catalina. What's yours?"

"Uh… Brandon."

"What are you doing here, Brandon?" She points to the plastic boot on my ankle. "You are hurt?"

"Yeah." I rub my eyes with the palms of my hand. *What time is it? Where did this girl come from?* "I mean, I hurt it yesterday, but I'm okay now. Mostly."

She leans back to get a better view of my ankle. Her short, straight hair falls over her face as she studies the plastic boot. "Does it hurt?"

Taking advantage of the extra space, I scoot a little to the side. *Oh, great. Now I'm pinned between a pile of horse manure and the little girl.* "It doesn't hurt much. I'm waiting for my brother and my cousin. They should be back any minute."

"Oh, you're one of Senora Sarah's boys."

"Yeah."

She takes in my one red high-top that is, of course, untied, my basketball shorts, my not-so-clean shirt, and then scans my face. "You should not be here, Brandon."

A tingle of apprehension zings across my shoulders. "What do you mean?" I glance at the still-blue sky. "It's not going to rain, is it?" *This is not someplace I should be sitting in a storm.*

"Where are Kyle and Trey?" *They should have been back ages ago.* "Are they okay?"

"Wait here. I will be back." With that, she skips around the bend in the canyon wall and disappears, leaving me with my raging imagination.

With my head cradled in my hands, I consider all the crazy things that have happened in the past few days. *Suburban Guy. The scrawny burglar. Mysterious maps. Secret passageways. Puzzle boxes and old-fashioned keys. And here I sit...alone...in a place called Smuggler's Gulch for crying out loud.*

I try to staunch the flow of wild possibilities that stampede through my thoughts. *Kyle and Trey have been kidnapped by Suburban Guy? Stumbled across an unmarked cavern and can't get out?* As the scenarios whirl in my imagination, I recognize my old enemy. Fear. Trying to slither in again.

Nope. Not this time. Lifting my eyes to the ribbon of blue sky overhead, I whisper, "Jesus, help. Keep my thoughts in line with your word." Peace settles over me, like an early morning mist over the lake back home, and Stan's song fills my thoughts. Humming the tune because I can't remember all the words, I lace my fingers behind my head and lean against the canyon wall. "And Jesus? Please bring Kyle and Trey back soon."

Moments later, the little girl appears around the bend, leading Kyle by the hand over a mound of rocks. Trey follows a few paces behind, munching on something. Something that smells really good.

"Where did you guys go? You've been gone forever!" My accusation bounces across the canyon walls and then fades into the wind. "Forever, ever, ever…"

Trey tilts his head at the echo and then hands over a bulging tortilla. With a louder-than-usual voice he says, "Here. I brought this for you." Trey grins as the echo of "For you, you, you…" bounces around the little canyon.

"For me? You were eating it!" I grab it from him. It's not like he hasn't slobbered on my food before.

"Well, yeah." Trey gives me a shrug. "It was dripping. I only ate the stuff that was falling out."

Catalina crouches beside me and studies me once again with those big, dark, long-lashed eyes. "You are hungry? Yes? This is *carne asada*, made by your friend, Emily."

"Emily? I thought she worked at a pizza place." I take a bite of the tender, seasoned beef wrapped in the flour tortilla. Now I understand why Trey couldn't resist.

"Brandon, we thought you were right behind us." Kyle starts to sit, and then discovers the pile of manure. "Hey! We were right. The horses have been coming through here."

"I was going to show you guys, but…" I take another bite of the burrito.

Kyle finds a horse-free spot and sits in the shade of the towering canyon. "We didn't realize you weren't right behind us until we stumbled into the camp."

"Stumbled is right." Trey rubs his shin and I see a nasty scrape with an already-forming bruise under his knee. "Literally." He plops onto the dirt beside Kyle.

Catalina giggles. "Everyone saw you."

While I chew and swallow, I'm trying to picture the scene that must have taken place. But I can't. "Camp? What are you talking about? I thought this led to a horse pasture."

Catalina repositions, crossing her legs into a pretzel and resting her bony elbows on her knees. She tilts her heart-shaped face into the palm of her hand as she watches me take another bite from the tortilla.

"Horse pasture, yes." Catalina nods. "But also, the camp where we live. "Us," she pats her chest. "The workers for Senora Sarah and…" a shudder ripples across her small shoulders, "the people with the horses."

"You can't see it from above," Kyle explains. "But there are a bunch of mobile homes along the edge of the pasture. The cliff hides it, I guess."

Trey nods. "Yeah. A barbed wire fence separates the horses and the camp. The fence is down in one spot. Somebody needs to fix that. Fast."

"Mmm uh," I agree through a mouthful of carne asada. Horses can get tangled up in barbed wire, and it's not good when they do.

"The people who work in the fields live in the mobile homes. Well, some of them, anyway. I don't know how many people live in the camp, but a lot. There were only a couple of moms there right now, and about a dozen kids." Trey glances at Catalina. "And Emily was there. With food."

"Emily is our friend." Catalina's snaggle-tooth smile lights up her brown face. "She brings food and makes games for the *ninos*."

"*Ninos*." I repeat the unfamiliar word. I should know what it means. "Children."

"Yes." Catalina gives me a good-job look. "Senora Sarah and Emily help the children and the mamas. Food, clean water, a generator for electricity. My family works for Senora Sarah. She is a good lady." The little girl lowers her voice. "But last year, before Senora Sarah was the boss…" Catalina looks around, as though afraid we're not alone in the quiet, sheltered canyon. "The bad men came last season when the mamas and papas were working. Right through here." She points across the gulley. "It is not good to be in the camp when the bad men come. Especially for the *ninos*."

Catalina unbends her legs and stands, her knobby knees now at my eye level. Shielding her eyes with her hand, she looks at the sky. "It's going to rain soon. We must go." She flashes a final smile over her shoulder. "*Adios*, Brandon. I hope your foot is better soon." Leaping like a deer over the pile of rocks, she disappears around the bend in the canyon.

We can hear her echoing footfalls as she skips to the camp on the other side of Smuggler's Gulch.

Chester is sitting at the edge of the cliff, watching as we make our way up the ravine. His ears are flat, and the tip of his tail is twitching. Kyle squats down and pats the grumpy cat. Chester glares at me from half-opened slits and turns his head away when I reach towards him.

"Chester, I'm sorry." *I can't believe I'm apologizing to a cat.* "We invited you. I thought you didn't want to come." Glancing at the stairs in the side of the cliff, I scoop Chester up. "Next time, I'll carry you, okay?"

Chester replies with a "murph" and a soft purr. Apparently, I'm forgiven. Chester settles into my lap for the ride home and I cringe when Kyle zips around a corner on two wheels. Chester's claws sink into my thigh, and I could swear the cat smirked.

Chapter 18

Trey stares at Kyle's phone and his face morphs into a look like he's about to hurl. Grabbing the red-padded bar on the side-by-side, I scoot forward and peer over the back of Trey's seat. I get a glimpse of the message icon at the bottom of Kyle's phone. With the number ten in a red circle above it.

"Uh oh." My stomach feels a little jittery now. "Aunt Sarah?"

"Texts from Aunt Sarah, Alex, Kyle's mom, and our mom. Plus, four voicemails that I haven't listened to." Trey bares his teeth in an emoji-like grimace. "We didn't have cell service until just now."

"Kyle, pull over." I smack his shoulder to get his attention. "Dude. We are in so much trouble. We have to call Aunt Sarah. And Mom. And *your* mom…"

At the mention of his mom, Kyle makes the same face Trey just did, and puts his foot on the brake. "We did kind of leave Aunt Sarah's in a hurry, didn't we?"

"After sending a text. We did send a text." Trey tosses the phone into Kyle's lap like it's too hot to touch. "It's *your* phone. You call them."

Kyle pleads at me with his eyes, but I hold my hands up and shake my head. "He's right. You're the only one with a cell phone, so …"

"Chicken." Kyle glares at me and then picks up the phone. "Both of you. Chickens." He hits the speaker button and plays the first voicemail. It's Aunt Sarah. And she's not happy.

"Boys? Where are you? Call me as soon as you get this message. I did get your text, and I can see from the hole in the fireplace that you found another tunnel, but I'm very concerned. Call me."

The next voicemail is from Alex. "Where are you guys? If we have to call the sheriff's department again, I'm going to pound all three of you. Call. Me. Back."

"Stop." Trey puts his hand on the phone before Kyle can play another message. "I don't want to hear any more. Just call Aunt Sarah and start apologizing."

Kyle's brown eyes dart from me to Trey, and then to the phone. With a resigned groan, he dials Aunt Sarah's number with the phone still on speaker. She picks up on the first ring. "Where are you? Are you okay? Are you boys all together?"

"Hey Aunt Sarah. Uh, we're fine. We were out of cell range and just now got your messages." He swallows hard. "All of your messages. And Mom's. And Aunt Jennifer's. And... uh, Alex's."

Trey chimes in, "We're all here. Brandon and Kyle and me. Oh, and Chester is with us. We're all fine."

"Where are you?"

Kyle glances at our surroundings before he answers. "We just left the cottonwood tree with the weird limbs. Right now, we're in the middle of...the Belair rows? I think." There's a long, staticky pause before Kyle fills the silence. "We'll be back to the house in a few minutes. Okay?"

"Okay." Aunt Sarah sighs, deep and heavy. "We'll talk when you get back."

"Is, uh, is Alex with you?"

"No. He's not." The edge on Aunt Sarah's voice shoots straight into my stomach, leaving me with a sharp, twisty feeling in my gut. "He's out searching for you. Along with everyone else."

"Oh." Kyle gulps. "Can you let him know we're on our way back?"

"No. You call Alex. I'll be busy notifying all the people searching for you. And contacting your parents, who are worried sick. Like I said, we'll talk when you get back."

Aunt Sarah disconnects the call without saying good-bye, and the silence that fills the air feels heavy. Trey is chewing his thumb again, and Kyle looks just like he did that time he swallowed a live goldfish. My stomach isn't happy either, but with an unexpected burst of boldness, I grab the phone.

"He's my brother. I'll do it." I scan through Kyle's contact list and hit Alex's name. As I wait for him to answer, I notice a battered blue pickup bouncing its way across the orchard. It's heading straight towards the side-by-side. "Kyle! Pull to the side. They can't get past if we're sitting in the middle of the row!"

Before Kyle can start the engine, the pickup is nose to nose with the ATV. Panic shoots through me as I realize that the fruit-laden trees have us blocked in. The only way out is in reverse, and I *really* don't think Kyle can pull that off.

The driver opens the door of the truck and steps onto the grassy path between the trees. His face is shaded by a ballcap that was red once upon a time, and even though I can't see his eyes, I feel his gaze on me. I'm so focused on the driver of the truck that I don't realize Alex has answered his phone.

"Guys? Hello? Can you hear me?"

"Alex?" My voice is shaky as I finally manage to spit out his name.

"Brandon, it's okay." Alex's voice crackles through the side-by-side. "Look straight ahead. It's me."

The passenger door of the pickup opens, and a wave of relief washes over me so strong I slump against the back of the seat as I disconnect the call. This might be the happiest I've ever been to see my older brother. Alex takes a few long strides across the uneven ground and then shakes his head as he stares us down with a look that could freeze a volcano. Chester puts his paws on the window and chirrs a greeting. *Sure, Chester's happy to see him. Me? Not quite as much as a second ago.*

Alex gives the cat a quick chin rub before he turns his attention to Kyle. "Out." Alex jabs his thumb over his shoulder and gives Kyle a death-glare. "Get out of the driver's seat."

"You're not going to leave me here!" Kyle's face turns pale. "Are you?"

"It *is* tempting." Alex hurries Kyle along with a tug on his shirt. "You can ride in the back with Brandon."

Scooting to the far corner, I make room for Kyle. He climbs into the back seat and Chester nestles between us.

Alex gives the driver of the pickup a thumbs up signal and hollers across the nose-to-nose vehicles. "Thanks for your help, Jose! Spread the word that the little troublemakers have been found. Hopefully we can get ahold of everyone before it starts to rain. See ya tomorrow." He turns to me and shakes his head as the engine rumbles to life. "You are in so much trouble."

Yeah, I know. But he doesn't have to look quite so happy about it.

Chapter 19

Hobbling from the carriage house and across Aunt Sarah's lawn takes all my concentration. Zings of pain shoot from my grape-fruit sized ankle to my knee. This is what Mom would call *consequences*. I've heard that lecture a time or two. I'm probably going to get Aunt Sarah's version in a minute. Whatever Aunt Sarah has to say, and no matter how loud she says it, I already know. I messed up. Big time.

Aunt Sarah holds the kitchen door open as I make my way to the house. Seeing the concern in her eyes makes me feel worse than the pain in my ankle. I try to wipe my feet on the rug but can't put my full weight on my right leg and can't lift my left foot while I'm standing on it.

"Don't worry about it, Brandon." The kindness in her voice makes me feel even worse. "A little mud on the floor is the least of our concerns right now."

Kyle and Trey follow me through the kitchen door. Aunt Sarah closes the door and slides the lock into place. "TV room, boys. Time for a talk."

We trudge to the TV room and the three of us drop onto the couch. I'm wedged in the middle, and nudge Kyle with my elbow. "Scoot over. I can barely breathe." I scooch the coffee table towards the couch and try not to wince as I put my feet on the battered wood surface.

Kyle notices my ankle. "Brandon! That looks bad."

I shift my weight onto my left hip. "I forgot my crutches when we left to find Smuggler's Gulch."

"Smuggler's Gulch?" Alex repeats with a frown. "What are you talking about *now*?"

Emily leans against the arched doorway. She folds her arms across her chest. "You should stay away from that place."

Aunt Sarah motions Emily into the room and the two of them spend a couple of minutes dragging chairs into position. Emily, Aunt Sarah and Alex settle into the semi-circle of armchairs, and their eyes bore into mine. Kyle and Trey fidget on either side of me.

With a sigh, I clench my hands into a ball of knuckles and dig my fingernails into my palms. *Okay, I'm ready. Let the Consequences Lecture begin.*

"First, let me just say," Aunt Sarah begins, "that I'm thankful that you're back safe and sound." With her arms resting on the chair, she steeples her fingers under her chin.

The lecture-pose. "However, leaving the house and taking the side-by-side without permission was not the best decision."

Aunt Sarah makes direct eye contact with each of us and as her eyes meet mine, I nod. *Yeah, I know. Not the best decision.*

"Under normal circumstances, I wouldn't have minded. Much." Aunt Sarah looks into my eyes again, and this time I see a spark of amusement.

Aunt Sarah holds my full attention with her flashing blue eyes.

"But we're not operating under normal circumstances. Agreed?"

With a glance at Trey and Kyle on either side of me, we all nod. Like bobble-heads. Which reminds me of the first night we were here, and the way Alex and I had nodded with the deputy after the break-in. The *first* break in.

Definitely not normal circumstances.

"With that in mind," Aunt Sarah moves her hands to her lap and squares her shoulders. "We need to discuss boundaries and expectations." She glances down, and I notice that her hands are clamped together in a knot almost like mine.

"I've called your parents and told them about everything that's happened. It's up to them to decide what happens next." Aunt Sarah chews her lip, something I've never seen her do before. She looks worn out. "If they decide you can stay for the rest of the month, then we need to set some ground rules."

"What do you mean, if?" Kyle scoots to the edge of the couch. "*If* we can stay? No! It was me. I was the one who talked Brandon and Trey into the whole thing."

I'm tempted to let Kyle take the blame. But I can't. With a half-smile, I put my hand on Kyle's shoulder. "That's not true, Kyle. Nobody forced us." I glance at my foot and add, "I was so excited I forgot to bring my crutches."

"And that's another thing," Aunt Sarah's tone was harsh now, and there was no lip-chewing when our eyes met this time. "Brandon, you're supposed to stay off of that foot until you see the specialist on Friday." Getting up from the chair, she strides across the room and peers at my ankle. "In fact, Alex, get the ice. If this continues to swell, we're going back to the emergency room."

I try to pull my foot off the table. "I hardly did any walking at all."

Aunt Sarah grips the sides of my ankle and holds it in place. "Leave it elevated." She unfastens the Velcro straps and slides the clunky contraption to the floor. "And take this off so the ice is more effective."

"You hardly did any walking." She mimics my words with a shake of her head. "Except for hiking down a steep incline and halfway into the canyon. And this was after tromping around the house and brawling with an intruder." Her face splits into that wonderful cascade of wrinkles as she lets out a chirp of laughter. "Your courage and fancy Judo-moves impressed the socks off of the deputies, by the way."

What? My courage? My shoulders feel a little broader, and I think I might have grown an inch or so in the past thirty seconds.

The goofy grin is wiped off my face when Alex plops a blue ice pack on my ankle. He also hands me a tiny plastic cup filled with liquid ibuprofen, and I thankfully gulp it down. My stupid ankle hurts like crazy. Emily hands us each a cold soda, and the hiss of popping tabs fills the room.

With Aunt Sarah, Emily and Alex once again seated in the armchairs, and the three of us squirming on the couch, the lecture portion of the afternoon continues.

"If your parents determine that you may stay for the month as planned, then we need to have clear rules." Aunt Sarah has her fingers steepled in the lecture-pose again.

"First, no ATVs without permission." She lifts her index fingers and taps them together. *Rule number one. Got it.*

She lifts another set of fingers. "Second, until the sheriff's department determines it's safe, you do not leave the house without permission." Aunt Sarah taps her middle fingers together, and it reminds me of that silly little-kid song about the church and the steeple. I try to hold back the inappropriate smirk, but she sees it.

"Brandon? Did you have something to add?"

"No ma'am." I lift my hands in a gesture of innocence. *Rule number two. Stay in the house. Understood.*

After determining that her stony stare has erased all inappropriate smirks, she continues. "Stan will install video doorbells on each entrance tonight, and Alex will help him install cameras on the outside of the house tomorrow."

Kyle scoots to the edge of the couch again. "Cool! You're getting the video doorbell?" He nudges me with his elbow. "We have that at our house."

"Yep," Aunt Sarah's expression softens again. "The orchard is barreling right into the twenty-first century, whether I'm ready or not." She taps her ring-fingers together in the finger- steeple. Only her pinkies remain of the finger-church. "The third rule…"

How does she do that? I attempt the same thing with my hands in my lap, but my ring-fingers aren't cooperating. *Huh. Must be all that piano playing.*

"Brandon? Are you paying attention?"

Shoving my hands under my legs, I shift my gaze to the blue ice pack balanced across my ankle. "Yeah. Third rule." Even though I'm staring at the ice pack, I can feel her eyes on me.

"Third rule," Aunt Sarah repeats. "Stay away from Smuggler's Gulch."

My head pops up and I open my mouth to protest, but before I can say a word, Emily leaps to her feet.

"Listen to your aunt." Emily wags her finger at our little row of troublemakers. "That is a very dangerous place. You don't go there anymore."

"Why?" Kyle asks.

I was wondering too.

Emily turns to Aunt Sarah, and some kind of unspoken communication passes between them before Emily answers, her finger once again wagging in our faces. "There are many reasons. To begin with, it's an arroyo. Do you know what that means?"

Trey and I just nod, but Kyle blurts out, "A dry creek bed."

Emily stares at her wagging finger, and then tucks her hands behind her back. "Yes, but not dry all the time. The rain we've had the past few days could turn that area into a raging torrent of water. It happens very quickly." She glances at Alex. "We saw it the other night."

"Yeah, we did." Alex pinches his nose, like the memory is giving him a headache. "It was a little scary.

"What if it's not raining?" Kyle asks. "Ow, Brandon! Don't poke me with your elbow. It's a legit question!"

See, this right here shows that he's an only child – more accustomed to *discussions* than *lectures* and asking questions in the middle of a you-are-in-so-much-trouble type of talk.

Kyle punches my arm. Hard. I have no choice but to hit him back.

Emily ignores the shoving match. "Smuggler's Gulch can be even more dangerous when it's not raining."

Kyle pauses in mid-punch and turns his attention back to Emily. "More dangerous? Why?"

Emily drops her eyes to the floor. "Because that's when the smuggler's use it."

All thoughts of punching Kyle evaporate. With my mouth hanging open, I look from Emily to Alex to Aunt Sarah. "For-real smugglers?"

Emily's intense, coffee-black eyes hold mine. "Real. And very bad."

"What do they smuggle?" Trey asks, and I feel his hand reach for mine.

We wait in frozen silence for what seems like forever before Aunt Sarah clears her throat. "We can discuss that later." She takes a deep breath. "Those are the three rules. Are they clear?"

"Yes, ma'am." We answer in chorus.

"Good." Aunt Sarah leans forward in her chair, and she rubs her hands together like she's putting on lotion. "Now, let's talk about the tunnels!"

Chapter 20

Just as Aunt Sarah opens the chance for us to spill details about the second tunnel, my stomach lets loose with a rumble that can be heard clear across the room. The burrito from Smuggler's Gulch is long gone, and I'm starving.

"On second thought," Aunt Sarah lifts her eyebrows and fights back a laugh. "Maybe we should have this conversation over dinner."

"What are we having for dinner?" Kyle pulls away from me, like I might poke him with my elbow again for asking another question.

"Anybody up for more *carne asada*?" Emily gives me a wink that sends a rush of heat across my face. *Why is it that every time she looks at me, I blush?*

"Is that the stuff we had in the workers camp?" Trey's eyes light up.

"Yeah, there was plenty, so I brought some for our dinner. It will just take a couple of minutes to get everything ready." Emily puts her hands on Trey's shoulder. "Trey, you and Kyle could help me in the kitchen, okay? While we're getting stuff ready, Brandon can stretch out on the couch." She smiles as she says this, but it doesn't hide the worried look in her eyes.

Trey and Kyle spring off the couch, eager to help. Maybe it's the food that appeals to them. But being around Emily isn't exactly a hardship.

Aunt Sarah hovers over me, lifting the ice pack and studying the effect it's had. My skin is pink from contact with the cold, but it's lost that angry, blotchy look. My ankle is now numb, and instead of grapefruit sized, it's down to a puffy-around-the edges look. *I guess that's good.*

"How's it feeling?" Aunt Sarah arranges a little stack of throw pillows at the end of the couch as she waits for my answer.

"It's okay." *Please stop fussing.*

She points to the stack of pillows. "You'll be more comfortable with your legs on the couch." That's more of a command than a suggestion.

"Okay." With my hands supporting the knee of my injured leg, I twist my hips and plop my ankles onto the pillows. Alex slips another pillow behind my shoulders as I lean against the arm of the couch. "Oh! Thanks." The thoughtful gesture startles me. *He must be worried, too. Again.*

Aunt Sarah secures the plastic boot on my ankle and tugs the Velcro into place. Stifling a yawn, I settle into the soft couch. My arms and legs feel heavy, and my head is sinking deep into the pillow. Just as I begin to close my eyes, my stomach lets out another roar. My eyes meet Aunt Sarah's, and we grin. There will be no naps until my stomach is happy.

"Dinner's ready!" Emily calls from the hallway. "Come and get it!"

"Wow, that was fast." Alex and I share a surprised look. He hands me the crutches.

"Uh, thanks." Aware of Alex's eyes following my every move, I swing my legs onto the floor, position the padded bars under my arms, and sniff the air. "That smells amazing."

When I hit the kitchen doorway, my stomach lets loose a rumble that everybody can hear. A white bowl, nestled on the blue-checked tablecloth between stacks of paper plates and napkins, fills the room with that incredible aroma. "I think *carne asada* is my new favorite thing," I announce to no one in particular.

"We could tell." Trey hands me a plate and then lifts the lid on a round tray. "Tortillas are in here, and the rest of the stuff is on the counter."

Aunt Sarah lays a hand on my arm. "First, let's pray."

I hold the empty plate against my chest and close my eyes. My stomach groans in protest at the delay. I hope it's a short prayer.

"Heavenly Father," Aunt Sarah's voice fills the room. "Thank you for all of the ways you have directed us, kept us safe, and watched over us today. Thank you for this food, and for all the ways you provide for us. Bless this food to our bodies and may the words we speak be a blessing to you. In Jesus name, amen."

Wasting no time, I load my plate and settle into a chair at the table. It doesn't take long for the rest of the group to do the same. Emily sets out a tray with some carrot sticks, sliced bell peppers, and cucumbers. She adds a little bowl filled with fresh guacamole to the table. *I could get used to this.* I'm munching my way through a second burrito when Stan knocks and pokes his head through the just-opened crack in the kitchen door.

"*Hola*! Can I come in?"

"Come on in!" Aunt Sarah motions to the table. "You're just in time for dinner."

Stan wipes his feet on the rug and then lifts his head to sniff the air. "You don't have to ask me twice. Smells great."

"It is great." Kyle says through a huge mouthful. "Your daughter is a good cook."

Stan turns a tap at the old-fashioned sink and squirts a blob of soap into his hands. "Oh, I know it." He rubs his hands together and then pauses, staring at the lather. "She's had a lot of practice. Too much for a girl her age." Flitting his hands beneath the streams of hot and cold water, he rinses the suds down the drain. "But she never complains."

"Now that we're all here," Aunt Sarah pushes her plate to the center of the table and settles back in the wooden chair. "Let's talk!" Her eyes sparkle, and everything about her looks brighter, more alive. Like she did before we got in trouble. "How did you figure out the secret entrance was in the fireplace?"

"Would you believe us if we told you it was Chester?" Kyle looks around for our black and white buddy. "Where is he, by the way?"

"Curled up beside the fireplace in the music room," Emily answers. "I think he's guarding the entrance. Or the exit." She shrugs. "I guess it depends on if you're inside or outside."

Aunt Sarah tilts her head to the side and smiles. "I *would* believe Chester had a paw in this discovery. After all, what would the Cousin Crew be without their faithful, furry friend?"

With the three of us talking at once, and with lots of interrupting, the story is told. The discovery of the peach blossoms on the map, the key that fit the slot with the double-blossom mark, and Chester's meows leading us to the secret panel in the fireplace.

"We got really excited." I try to explain. "And that's how we ended up in the side-by-side. And we're really sorry about all of that."

Aunt Sarah wags a finger. "That's already been discussed. Just follow the three rules, right? Now, tell me about your theory, Kyle, and how you ended up in Smuggler's Gulch."

Scooting to the edge of his seat, Kyle reports finding the painting at Big Jim's, and the tree with the twisted limbs that led him to the stairs carved into the stony cliff. "And that's how we knew it's called Smuggler's Gulch, and that's how we ended up in the worker's camp." Kyle ends the story with a dramatic ta-da arm motion.

Alex looks around the kitchen with a frown. "Hey, where is the map?"

Kyle had it at the cottonwood tree. He disappeared over the edge of the cliff. And that's the last I remember seeing it. "Oh no." My voice is a combination between whimper and groan. "We left it at the tree."

Emily stands and begins to clear the food from the table. "You did leave it at the cottonwood tree." With an ornery glimmer in her dark eyes, she lifts her eyebrows. "Thank goodness I followed you home."

"You found it?" Kyle leaps to his feet, knocking over the chair. "You brought it with you?"

With a twist of her shoulder, Emily flips her hair away from her face. "I did. And it wasn't easy." She nods towards the almost-empty white bowl. "My hands were already a little full."

Trey rushes to Emily and wraps her in an enthusiastic hug. "Thank you!" As if he suddenly realizes what he's doing, he drops his arms and stammers out, "I mean… uh…we forgot it was there, so thank you for picking it up." His face is volcano-red. *Poor Trey. I know exactly how he feels.*

"The map is in the music room."

Kyle puts his chair back into an upright position, and without being told, begins to scoop up the used paper plates and napkins. Emily and Alex tidy up the non-throw-away dishes while Stan puts the remaining food in plastic containers. Trey hoists the bulging trashcan liner from the metal can by the sink and lugs it closer to Kyle. I can tell he doesn't want to take the trash out to the dumpster by himself. In the dark.

"Brandon?" Aunt Sarah hovers over my shoulder. "How's the ankle? Let's look at the swelling."

Scootching the chair away from the table, I stand on my good leg and twist the chair a quarter turn. I plop back into the seat and stretch the boot towards her. "It's good. The swelling is better."

Not taking my word for it, she kneels on her haunches and unfastens the Velcro tabs. She presses the sides of my ankle. Left side. Right side. Top. Bottom. Her finger leaves white impressions, and together, we watch the color slowly return to each mark.

"Is it painful?"

"Not as bad as before."

"Well, that's encouraging." Aunt Sarah stares at my leg for a few seconds and then tugs the straps back around my ankle. "How's that? Too tight?"

"It's fine."

Aunt Sarah studies my face for a moment. "You're a tough kid. But hear this: you are going to stay in the house, and off that leg until the appointment with the specialist on Friday. And if you don't, you're going home. Immediately. Understood?

"Yes ma'am." *Yikes*.

Stan has finished putting the food away, and as he wipes his hands on the towel by the sink, he nods to Kyle. "I hear you're pretty good with computers."

Understatement alert! Leaning around Aunt Sarah, I see Kyle at the kitchen door, one hand pushing the door open and the other lugging the trash bag.

Kyle pauses at the door. "Pretty good, yeah."

"Computers aren't my best thing," Stan walks to the door and holds it open for Kyle. "I was thinking, maybe you can help me and Alex with the video doorbells?"

Kyle's eyes flicker and I can tell he's excited, but his voice is low-key like he doesn't care one way or the other. "Sure. That'd be cool."

"Great." Stan flicks the switch beside the door, and I don't know which shines brighter, the porch light, or Kyle's grin.

Chapter 21

The kitchen table is loaded down with tools. Alex, Stan and Kyle are absorbed with the details of installing the video doorbell system. When chords from the piano drift into the kitchen, Trey and I wander towards the sound of the music. Aunt Sarah lifts one hand to greet us while continuing to play the song with the other hand. *How does she do that?*

"Come on in! What would you like to hear?"

We step into the room, exchanging a glance and a shrug. My mind is blank. I can tell by the look in Trey's eyes that he's not pulling up any ideas either. Chester lifts his head and yawns from his cozy spot in a chair. I plop onto the fancy blue couch. It takes a lot of wiggling before I find a comfortable position, and I eye Chester's chair with a little envy. But the cat *was* here first.

The marble tiles have been moved back into place, and the mess we left behind has been cleaned up. Other than

Chester's charcoal-smudge paw prints on the floral rug, you'd never know we'd discovered another secret passage.

Trey hovers over Aunt Sarah's shoulder, mesmerized by the way her hands dance across the keys. With her right hand still playing the melody, she pats an empty spot on the bench with her left hand. "Sit down, Trey. If you're interested, I can teach you how to play a duet with me."

"A duet?"

"Two people playing at the same time." She wiggles her eyebrows. "Wanna give it a try?"

"I guess so, yeah." Trey slides onto the bench beside her.

It takes a few minutes of plinking and plunking, and then Trey's picking out his part and Aunt Sarah's playing her part. They're not going to be on *America's Got Talent* anytime soon, but not bad for a ten-year-old kid with five minutes of practice. I close my eyes as Trey taps out the melody of *This Little Light of Mine*. Aunt Sarah adds some chords and I realize my toe is tapping along with the familiar song.

Short bursts of scenes from the day play over and over in my head, with the piano duet in the background like a crazy music video. *Puzzle-box. Scrap of paper. Map. Break-in Guy on the floor. Tunnels. Spider webs. Smuggler's Gulch. Cottonwood tree.*

And then I remember the first night. *Broken window. Broken pottery. First Break-in Guy. Missing pottery jug.*

"Hey, guys?" Sitting straight up, I startle Chester, who raises his head and glares at the interruption of his nap.

Aunt Sarah pauses, her hand hovering over the keyboard as our eyes lock. It takes Trey a moment longer to stop playing, and the tinkly echo of his last note drifts across the room.

Now that I have their attention, I ask the question that just came to me. "Did we ever find the missing pottery jug?"

Aunt Sarah shakes her head. "I looked everywhere I could think of, but I can't find it."

"I don't think Suburban Guy is after the map at all."

Trey gives me a look that makes me wonder about my sanity. But I know I'm onto something. "Trey, go get those pottery jugs from upstairs."

"Yes sir!" Trey gives me a salute and turns on his heel like a Marine. "Be right back, sir!" He marches out of the room with his arms swinging.

I move from the fancy blue couch to the floor just as Trey returns with a jug in each hand. Kyle, Alex, Emily and Stan follow behind him in a curious line. Trey bends at the waist and holds them in front of my nose. "The pottery jugs, Your Bossiness, sir."

Sighing, I take one in each hand. "Thank you, Trey." *See? I have manners!*

Aunt Sarah puts her hand on the blue couch and slowly eases onto the floor beside me. "What is it, Brandon?"

Before I can answer, everyone else crowds around, trying to get a good view.

"Give me some room, people!" I make a shoving motion and wait until everyone has scooted back a little. "And you, buddy," I heft the cat off the map. "Go sit with Kyle." With a glance at Trey, I add, "Please."

"Oh, sure." Trey gives an exaggerated sigh. "You say please to the cat."

Running my finger along the saddle-shaped spout of the first jug, I study the shape and weight of the container. *Similar. Not exactly the same.* I pick up the second pitcher and compare the weight.

Handing them to Aunt Sarah, I ask, "Am I imagining things, or do you notice a difference between the two?"

She frowns and tips her head to the side as she takes a pitcher in each hand. "I always thought they were the same." Her eyebrows raise into the stratosphere. "Oh. I see what you mean." She tilts the pottery in her left hand, and studies the thick, flat bottom. "This one is heavier. And the bottom is different."

Kyle holds his index finger against the base of the first jar. "This jug has a one-finger-width-high base." He places his finger against the same spot on the second jar. "The bottom of this one is two-finger-widths high." He frowns "Is that what you mean?"

"That's exactly what I mean."

"So what?" Alex sits beside me. "They're hand-made. They're going to be different."

"That's what I thought. Until I remembered what Break-in Guy said on the phone. He said he grabbed the wrong one. I think he took a pottery jug. That's why Aunt Sarah can't find it."

"The one with the green stripes," Aunt Sarah says. "But why?"

"You got these from your kids, right?"

"Miguel gave me the four pottery jugs, but said they were from all the kids."

"I think he hid something in the jars. Something he wanted to give you but was trying to hide from someone else."

"But what? The kids didn't have…" Aunt Sarah's face turns an ashy color. "Miguel's uncle. He tried to convince Miguel to join the family business instead of continuing at school." She uses finger quotes around family business, and says the words like they taste bad. "Miguel was really upset after his uncle's visit. His uncle is a very bad man."

"See this ridge on the bottom of the jug?" My thumbnail just fits into the space. "And this jar is heavier than the other one."

"You think something is hidden there?"

Stan pulls a pocketknife from his pocket. "Let me see that, Brandon." He sits next to me on the floor. Stan jiggles the edge of the knife into the space my thumbnail had discovered. Slowly, he removes the bottom of the jug.

Trey tilts his head at the faint tinkling sound. "It sounds like plastic beads."

"I don't think these are plastic." Kyle's voice is barely above a whisper as the cascade of green stones clatters onto the marble tiles.

Aunt Sarah stares at the stones as if they're poisonous. "Those are uncut emeralds." She covers her mouth with her hand. "I've seen one or two before. But never this many."

Stan says, "Those must be worth a fortune. How did Miguel get them?"

Aunt Sarah rubs her hands over her face. "My guess? His uncle." She uses finger quotes again as she adds, "The family business." She shakes her head and sighs. "Illegal drugs, weapons, I knew about those sides of it. But this," she waves her hand across the heap of glittering green stones. "This is a surprise."

"How would kids have gotten ahold of these, though?" I'm trying to wrap my brain around it all.

"When I decided it was time to leave Colombia, our mission organization found a couple from Canada to take over the orphanage. But their paperwork to get into the country was delayed. A group of Catholic nuns at a nearby convent agreed to take the children until the new couple arrived. Any living relatives of our children were notified.

"Two days before I was scheduled to leave, Miguel's uncle showed up. He tried to convince Miguel and a few of the older boys to leave school and work for him. He promised to pay them a lot of money. Who knows what else he used to try and persuade them?" Aunt Sarah's eyes get that far-away look.

"Miguel was alone in the village with his uncle for an hour or so, and when he came back, he was upset. Miguel asked the nuns to lock the gate to the convent. He was afraid his uncle might not take no for an answer. Not everyone in his uncle's organization joins voluntarily."

"The next day, Miguel gave me the pottery." Aunt Sarah rubs her finger along the edge of the now-bottomless jug. "He told me that all of the children wanted me to have these to remember them by."

Emily picks up one of the green stones and holds it to the light. "Have you heard from Miguel since you've been back in the States?"

"He wrote me a letter a few weeks ago. He plans to begin classes at university in the fall."

"So, he's safe?" Emily asks as she lays the stone back on the floor.

Aunt Sarah's forehead crinkles. "As far as I know, yes."

"Did Uncle Joe ever tell the kids in Colombia stories about growing up in Colorado? I mean, he used to tell Mom and Aunt Bekki stories about this place. Did he tell your kids, too?"

Aunt Sarah bites her bottom lip and her eyes flit to the ceiling. "Maybe." Looking down once again, she says, "I was always so busy with the little ones. Now that I think about it, Joe could have used the tale of his smuggler-grandfather as an example of how he didn't let his family's past determine his future." She smiles. "That was one of his favorite sayings: When you become a follower of Jesus, your future is no longer defined by your past. You have a new identity as a child of God."

As Aunt Sarah talks, I run my fingers across the green stones. Thoughts are crashing through my head like four-year-olds in a bouncy-castle.

"Aunt Sarah, did you ever meet Miguel's uncle?" I ask.

"Now that you mention it," Aunt Sarah tilts her head. "No. I never did."

I blurt out the crazy idea that just popped into my head. "I think Suburban Guy is Miguel's uncle. And he wants his emeralds back."

"But what about the map?" Kyle demands.

"And the puzzle box?" Trey asks.

"And the secret tunnels?" Alex adds with a shudder. "Don't forget the creepy secret tunnel that opens into my bedroom."

"What about Big Jim's painting with the cottonwood tree that led you to Smuggler's Gulch?" Emily crosses her arms across her chest. "That can't be a coincidence."

"A few minutes ago, Aunt Sarah and Trey were playing the piano. And I was thinking about all the random, unconnected things that have happened over the last couple of days." I rub my hand across the back of my neck. "Only, they're all connected."

Taking a deep breath, I try to put my jumbled thoughts into words. "When I was in the tunnel, the first tunnel, there weren't spiderwebs. Maybe a couple, but not many." I look at the faces around me. Everyone's looking at me like I'm a little nutzo. "But this tunnel, or secret entrance, or whatever we're calling it…" I point to the fireplace. "This one was loaded with spiderwebs."

Reaching a hand to Chester, I run my hand along his fuzzy back. "This guy knew about both of these places." Silent nods of agreement encourage me to go on. "Nobody bigger than a cat has used this one for ages." I nod towards the fireplace. "We can tell because of the spider webs."

"That's true." Kyle scratches Chester under the chin. "The first tunnel did seem pretty clean. For a tunnel."

"Yeah," Trey agrees. "I guess that is kinda weird."

"Which means that *somebody* has been in that tunnel recently. Right?"

Alex lets out a low whistle and a shudder ripples through his body. "That is not a comforting thought." He rubs his arms.

"Then we've got the Jones place and the painting of Smuggler's Gulch." I point a finger at Emily. "Catalina told me that sometimes bad men came. She said it was dangerous to be in Smuggler's Gulch, especially for the *ninos*." Emily drops her gaze to the floor. I take this to mean I'm onto something, so I keep going with my crazy theory.

"The worker's I've met all love you, Aunt Sarah. But they clam up when anybody mentions the Jones' vineyard. Even Catalina. They all seem afraid. But I don't know what they're afraid of, exactly."

Stan clears his throat and takes a deep breath. "You're right, Brandon. The workers *are* afraid. The Jones family hired a foreman a couple of years ago. Their daughter was sick, and they needed to be with her while she was going through treatment. Since that guy has been in charge, some strange things have been happening. Trucks come and go at night, and people are in and out that don't seem to have jobs related to the vineyard. It's suspicious, but that's about all I know."

Stan moves to sit beside Emily and puts an arm across her shoulder. "One of the biggest reasons the workers are scared is this; last harvest season, three kids and their mom disappeared one afternoon. Nobody was sure if she left because she wanted to, or if something worse happened."

"Like what?" Kyle asks with a frown. "Like they fell in the river and drowned?"

Stan shrugs. "That's one possibility. The Search and Rescue team spent several days looking for them but never found a trace. Another possibility is that they were taken somewhere against their will. There are bad people that will pay money for kidnapped women and children. It's called human trafficking."

"So, they sell them? To be slaves?" Kyle's eyes are wide. "That's horrible!"

Emily is blinking back tears.

Waiting until her eyes meet mine, I ask, "That's why you told us to stay away from Smuggler's Gulch?"

"Yes." Emily's voice is husky. "I knew the woman who disappeared. She was my friend." Emily chews her lip for a moment before she adds, "I've seen the men at the Jones vineyard, and they scare me."

Emily picks up a handful of green stones and then places them in a line on the floor. The light dances across the gems, and I can't help but stare. *Are they worth a lot of money?*

Rubbing the last gem with her finger, Emily looks up, and our eyes meet again. "Adding to your theory Brandon, maybe the man trying to buy Sarah's property *is* Miguel's uncle. Maybe he knows about the tunnel. He could sneak all kinds of things – or people, in and out through that tunnel and nobody would know."

Aunt Sarah puts her hand over her mouth. "How would he know about the secret entrance?"

I pipe up. "If Uncle Joe told the kids stories about the house he grew up in, maybe Miguel accidentally told his uncle. My mom thought Uncle Joe made up the stories just for fun. Maybe Miguel did too?"

Aunt Sarah shakes her head. "I don't know. That's a lot of maybes."

"Why would the uncle come to the United States, though?" Trey chews his thumb. "Palisade, Colorado is a long way from Colombia."

Kyle touches the little pile of green stones. "This might be a pretty big reason. How much do you think these are worth, Aunt Sarah?"

"I have no idea." She lays a few glittery green rocks in the palm of her hand. "This one is so clear I can see right through it. And it's such a deep shade of green. This might be very valuable." She shrugs. "Or it might just be a pretty piece of glass to put in an aquarium. An expert gemologist would have to look at them."

"Do you know an expert gemologist?" Kyle asks.

"Nope." Aunt Sarah laughs. "I've never needed one. Until now."

Trey yawns and rubs his eyes with the back of his hand. I saw him yawn, and that makes me fight one of my own. Aunt Sarah takes that as her cue.

"Time to wrap this up for tonight. It's been quite a day."

"But what are we going to do with these?" I point to the green stones scattered across the floor.

"Here," Emily hands Aunt Sarah a sandwich-sized food storage bag. "It's not fancy, but…"

"That will work." Aunt Sarah scoops the stones into the bag. She slides the little red zipper and shakes it to make sure it's sealed, then hands it to Stan. "And Stan will put them in the safe."

"You have a safe?"

"Up until now, I've only kept a few important papers in it."

"But what if the bad guys try to break in again?"

Stan answers as he takes the plastic bag. "Video cameras are up and running, the alarm is set, and Emily and I are staying here tonight. I think we've got it covered."

"But –

Aunt Sarah puts up her hand in a stop gesture. "Tomorrow we can figure out what to do with the emeralds. If that's what they even are." She stifles a yawn of her own and adds, "But, right now, it's time for baths. And then off to bed."

We moan and struggle to our feet. With one last glance at the bag in Stan's hand, I trudge with Trey and Kyle towards the stairs.

Sniffing my freshly washed arm pits, I stretch out in the bed and stare at the Texas-shaped stain on the ceiling. *Are those Colombian emeralds? Is that what Suburban Guy has been after? Why is there a map of the secret tunnels?* I'm too sleepy to think about it anymore tonight. With an epic yawn, I close my eyes and settle into the pillow. I barely notice when Trey and Kyle scoot in on either side of me. When Chester thunks onto the bed, I curl onto my side so he can nestle behind my knees.

Chapter 22

The next thing I know, sunlight streams through the window as Chester pats my chin with his paw. "Chester, no."

No sign of Trey and Kyle, other than a tangle of blankets and a pillow on the floor. Chester hops onto my chest and tugs his scratchy tongue across my cheek. "Ouch!" His fish-breath blasts over me and I surrender with a groan. "Fine. I'm up."

Satisfied that I'm upright and moving, Chester settles into the pillow, still warm from my body heat.

Rummaging through my suitcase, I pull out a clean shirt. The basketball shorts I wore yesterday are wadded into a ball on the floor. After a quick sniff inspection, I decide they could use a run through the washing machine and throw them back into the corner. Chester hops to the floor while I struggle into a pair of cargo shorts. With his tail high, he leads me down the stairs and to the kitchen.

The middle of the table holds a pitcher of orange juice, an almost-empty bowl of scrambled eggs and a plate with a couple of pancakes. I reach for the pancakes as the grandfather clock in the hallway chimes the hour. Eight chimes.

"About time." Kyle slurps the last of his orange juice and plunks his used dishes into the sink.

"Yeah." Trey joins Kyle at the sink. "It's eight o'clock, and you're just getting up."

My eyes feel gritty, and I fight back a yawn as I pour a glass of juice. *I would have stayed in bed for another hour or two if it weren't for the alarm-cat.* "Where is everyone?" I load my plate with the last of the scrambled eggs and spear the pancakes with my fork. The eggs are cold but warming them up in the microwave seems like too much effort.

"Alex and Stan are working on the roof. Emily is at work." Kyle squirts dish soap onto the pile of dishes.

"Aunt Sarah's making a phone call." Trey looks through the window above the sink. "She said that after yesterday, she's sticking to us like glue."

Shoving a forkful of room-temperature pancake into my mouth, I nod. Yesterday *was* a little crazy. I can't believe our parents are letting us stay. *Are they letting us stay?*

Swallowing the last of the pancakes, I add my plate to the bubbles. "I sure would like another look in that tunnel today. Before our parents make us go home."

Trey's freckles scrunch into a wrinkled line across his nose. "I don't want to go home yet." He grabs a plate from Kyle and rubs the towel across the surface before setting it in the rack.

"Yeah," Kyle hands Trey another plate, dripping suds onto the floor. "Me too."

Aunt Sarah walks into the room. "Brandon, you're going to stay off that foot today. We have one day until your appointment with the specialist, and by golly, you're going to take it easy until then."

Sitting around the house all day doing nothing sounds terrible. "What if I sit on the ground while I work on the flower bed? That's taking it easy *and* being helpful, right?"

With a chirp of laughter, she nods her head. "I can't argue with that. As long as you stay off that foot."

"We'll help you, Brandon." Kyle hangs the dish towel on the rack. "We should get started before it gets too hot."

Aunt Sarah follows us to the flower bed. The trowels and wheelbarrow are right where we left them – on the lawn between the carriage house and the kitchen door. If Mom were here, I'd be getting a well-deserved chewing out about now.

I step around the wobbly pickets to the knee-high grass on the other side of the fence. "I'll work on this side, and you guys can do that side of the fence, okay?"

"Fine by me," Trey plops onto the ground. "Are these weeds or flowers?" He points to a spiky green plant.

Aunt Sarah bends to get a better look. "I'm not really sure." She scratches her cheek. "Go ahead and pull it."

I leave Trey and Kyle to their weed pulling and turn my attention to the pickets of the old fence. Yanking a fistful of clingy weeds away from the weathered wood, I spot a curved piece of stone.

"Hey, check this out! I think there's a stone bench over here."

Aunt Sarah kneels beside me. "It is! If we pull some of these weeds, we can set it upright." Together we tug grass and vines away from the stone. "What's this?" Aunt Sarah taps the tip of her trowel onto something with a clunk.

"Did you find another bench?" Trey pops his head over the waist high fence to get a better look.

"We found something buried under the bench." Aunt Sarah's voice quivers. "Maybe that map was about more than just tunnels, huh?" She sits on the ground. "It's probably nothing. My imagination is running wild." She laughs. "Oh, my goodness. You do it." She hands me the trowel.

"Do it, Brandon." Trey jumps from one foot to the other. "The suspense is killing me!"

Kyle punches his arm. "Or you have to pee." He grins. "Either way, hurry Brandon!"

Maybe this really is a buried-treasure kind of house! My heart pounds like a bongo drum as I shove the trowel into the ground. Dirt flies through the air as the hole gets deeper. The scrape of metal-on-metal ripples through me like electricity. Tossing the little shovel to the side, I brush the dirt with my fingers to reveal a rusty metal box.

Aunt Sarah grabs the trowel and uses it to pry the container away from the hard-packed soil. "It's an old cracker tin!" With a grunt, she lands on her bottom, the container clutched to her chest.

We stare, unsure of what to do. *Is she hurt? Should I offer her a hand?*

And then Aunt Sarah erupts into laughter. I don't mean dainty, dignified giggles. No; this is snorting, rib-crunching laughter. And it's contagious. We're all laughing – tears streaming down our cheeks, barely able to breathe.

Until a shadow falls across our merry little group, and we look up. Stunned silence fills the peach scented air. Even the birds stop chirping as the hot summer air becomes thick with dread.

Giant-Driver-Guy looms over us, his rock-hard biceps flexing as he stares us down. Suburban-Guy stands a couple of steps behind him, intimidation shooting from his glittery bird-eyes. I tear my focus away from his face, feeling like a rabbit under the gaze of a circling hawk. The all-black Suburban is parked at the far end of the driveway. I didn't even hear it.

"We'll take that." The driver reaches his tattoo-swirled arm towards Aunt Sarah.

"Oh no, you won't." Aunt Sarah pops to her feet and slams the canister into Kyle's stomach like a seasoned football center snaps the ball to the quarterback. "Run, Kyle. Tunnel B. Go!"

Kyle hugs the cracker tin to his chest and bolts across the lawn.

Without taking her eyes away from the intruders, Aunt Sarah touches Trey's shoulder. "You too. Scoot!"

Trey leaps over the rickety fence and races after Kyle. They slam through the kitchen door and disappear into the old house. I hope they remember to slide the deadbolt into place.

Movement catches my eye, and I glance up. Stan's face is just visible from the gable over the kitchen door. He puts a finger to his lips and then disappears from my line of sight. I don't know how he got there, or what he's planning, but I turn back towards our unwelcome guests with more confidence than I had a second ago.

"Mrs. Hooper, you are being most difficult. Again." The boss-guy's accented voice cuts into the silence. "You force me to become unpleasant." He's been standing with his arms behind his back, and as he lifts his hand, I see a gun.

The kind bad guys use in the movies. The barrel aimed at my chest.

My heart can't decide if it should go to marathon-speed or stop pumping all together. My hands are clammy. I'm fighting for breath. *Will I see the bullet? How bad will it hurt?*

Then a different thought pops into my head. *God has not given us a spirit of fear, but of power, love and a sound mind.* My heart rate slows. I let out a slow breath.

Power. Love. Sound mind.

I glance at Aunt Sarah. She plants her feet in the dirt and crosses her arms across her chest. Ready for battle. "In the name of Jesus, put that gun away."

The complete absence of fear radiates off her like heat waves. The man frowns, as if confused. Blinking in surprise, he lowers the gun.

What is happening?

Aunt Sarah's eyes narrow as she studies the man with the gun. "I know who you are."

"Yes, I have been here. Offering to buy your property."

"You were also here the night my house was broken into. But I know who you are. You are the uncle of Miguel Rodriguez." She follows this statement with a flurry of Spanish words.

Suburban Guy nods. "Si."

While the Spanish conversation rolls over my head, I glance at the house. *Are Kyle and Trey in the hiding place? Where are Stan and Alex?*

When I turn back, the driver is taking a step backwards, looking uncertainly at his boss. Aunt Sarah steps forward, still speaking rapid-fire Spanish, and shakes her finger at the enormous man as if he's a naughty child.

Two sheriff's department vehicles churn up the drive with a little chirp of the siren. The tattooed giant lifts his hands and puts them on his head, then drops to his knees.

The deputies park with the noses of their vehicles pointing together, forming an arrow-shaped barrier across the driveway. Four burly deputies tumble out of the vehicles with hands on their holstered weapons. Deputy Chavez barks orders in Spanish, and before I even realize what's happening, the uncle is on the ground, with Deputy Chavez' knee holding him in place. A deputy I haven't seen before slips the gun into a plastic bag as Chavez pulls handcuffs from a pouch on his belt.

Alex and Stan make it down from their perch on the roof in time to watch the handcuffing. A regular-sized deputy looks like a little kid playing dress up as he clips handcuffs onto the tattooed driver. Once the intruders are in the back of the vehicle, we tromp across the dug-up yard to the house.

Chapter 23

"How'd you guys get here so fast?" I ask Deputy Chavez.

"We've had extra patrols in place for the past few days. Stan called us when he saw the Suburban turn off the highway. He had a bird's eye view from the roof."

Chester rubs across my legs as I peer into the fireplace. "Trey? Kyle? You can come out. The bad guys are gone." Trey's eye blinking through a tiny crack in the marble is the only thing that gives away their hiding place.

Kyle and Trey pull spider webs from their hair and clothes the entire time we go through the all-too-familiar drill of statements and explanations for Deputy Chavez. His eyes just about bug out of his head when he sees the stash of emeralds from the pottery jug.

"What's in the cracker tin?" Deputy Chavez eyes the rusty container that Kyle is still holding in his lap. "More emeralds?"

"We haven't opened it yet, "Aunt Sarah answers. "After last night's discovery, I have no idea what to expect from a container that's been buried in a flower bed for years." Sarah nods to Kyle. "Let's open it and see, shall we?"

The lid is rusted in place, and it takes some WD-40, a flat-head screwdriver, and some determination before the lid finally pops off. When Kyle pulls out a piece of burlap, a moan of disappointment echoes across the room.

"Keep digging," Aunt Sarah nudges Kyle. "That could be just a protective cover."

Kyle's eyes go wide and his mouth pops open as he shoves his hand towards the bottom of the can.

Trey tilts his head at the clattering sound. "Is that more emeralds?"

"Nope. Not emeralds." Kyle dumps the canister on its side, and we all gasp at the mound of silver and gold coins that tumble onto the floor.

"This one is dated 1929!" Deputy Chavez holds it up to the light. "In mint condition. This might be worth quite a bit to a collector."

"Oh my gosh!" Trey leaps to his feet and scuttles into the fireplace hiding spot. He hurries back a moment later with another cracker tin in his arms. "While we were hiding from the bad guys just now, I found this. It was stuffed into a corner."

"Do you think it's more coins?" Kyle squirts a little WD-40 on the lid and wiggles the screwdriver under the ridge. "Why would anyone hide coins in cracker tins?"

The lid loosens with a pop, and Kyle lets out a low whistle. "It's more coins! These look really old." He picks one up. "1904."

Aunt Sarah paces across the floor. "People didn't trust banks after the crash in 1929, so I suppose Joe's grandfather might have buried his savings. Or, if he really was a bootlegger, he might've hidden his ill-gotten gains, huh?" She turns to Deputy Chavez. "Are these legally mine?"

"I'm not positive, but since you own the land, I think the answer is yes." He points to the second cracker tin. "This was inside your home. And you're the official heir of the property. Legally, yep. It's yours."

"What about the emeralds?" Aunt Sarah chews a fingernail. "Can I keep them?"

He shrugs. "Talk to your attorney. This is way outside of my area of knowledge, but if it was up to me, I'd rather see you keep them than the leader of a drug cartel. You'll have to pay taxes on everything of course."

"Of course." Aunt Sarah smiles at Stan. "Even without the emeralds, I think we can afford that new roof after all."

Chapter 24

This is it. My appointment with the specialist is in an hour.

Kyle sits next to me on the steps of the front porch. "Are you nervous?"

"A little," I admit. "I know a kid in Lake City that broke his foot. They did surgery on him, and he was in a wheelchair for the entire summer. A wheelchair!"

Kyle punches my arm. "You won't need surgery. And you for sure won't need a wheelchair."

"I hope you're right." My eyes scan the tree-lined driveway. Mom will be here any minute. "What if I messed something up yesterday?"

"You didn't." Kyle sounds confident. "It's not even swollen this morning. And you didn't cry in your sleep last night."

"I don't cry in my sleep!"

"You did the first night." He shrugs. "I'm really sorry about the flashlight thing, Brandon."

I catch a glimpse of Mom's Jeep through the trees, and struggle to my feet. "Kyle, for the last time, it wasn't your fault. Okay?"

Mom throws open the door of the SUV and runs towards me. "Brandon!" She swoops me into a hug and squeezes so hard I can't breathe.

With her arm around my shoulder, we head up the rickety stairs. "Tell me everything. Secret tunnels. Stashes of treasure. Bad guys from Colombia." She leans away from me and studies my face. "And you! Putting all the pieces together. Impressive, kiddo."

"Jennifer!" Aunt Sarah opens the front door with a happy smile. "So good to see you. I'm sorry it's under less-than-ideal circumstances." She pulls Mom into one of her lung-crushing hugs.

As we step through the front door, Mom says, "I knew if *anyone* could handle the Cousin Crew for a month, it would be you, Aunt Sarah. But I didn't expect these kinds of adventures."

"It has been a little exciting over the past few days." Aunt Sarah leads us into the kitchen. "And I can't wait to tell you all about it. But we need to get Brandon to his appointment."

"Don't tell her anything without us!" Trey charges into the kitchen and launches himself at Mom. She staggers to a chair, and he scoots into her lap like a little kid. "Mom, don't let them tell you anything unless I'm here, okay?"

"Okay." Mom runs her hand through Trey's sandy hair. "Not a word about it unless you're in the room." Mom closes her eyes and inhales. "I've missed you, Peanut."

Only a mom would deliberately sniff a stinky little kid.

"But right now, we'd better get rolling. Brandon's got a date with a specialist." Mom leans around Trey and scans the kitchen. "Where's Alex?"

"He and Stan went to the hardware store." Aunt Sarah motions Emily into the room. "Jennifer, I'd like you to meet Emily. I couldn't run this place without Emily and her father's help."

"A pleasure to meet you," Mom says, dumping Trey onto the floor. "And thank you for hanging out with the boys this morning."

"Glad I can help." Emily puts her hands on Trey's shoulders. "Trey let's go work on that flower bed. Maybe we can have it done by the time they get back."

Trey jumps to his feet. "Maybe we'll find another tin full of old coins!" He bellows at the top of his lungs, "Kyle! Flower garden! C'mon!" Before he charges through the kitchen door, he hollers over his shoulder, "Bye, Mom!"

Emily shakes her head and follows Trey. She pauses at the door. "It was nice to meet you, Jennifer. Good luck at the doctor, Brandon."

Resting the hard plaster cast across the back seat of the Jeep, I close my eyes and lean against the door. The smell of ripening peaches increases as the SUV climbs the hill. *Walking cast for six weeks. I can do that.* And Mom is letting me stay with Aunt Sarah for the rest of the month! It's the best possible outcome. "Thank you, Jesus," I whisper.

Mom parks the Jeep and I swing my new cast out of the backseat and onto the gravel. It feels weird. Heavy. Stiff. *I can do this.*

Clomping towards the house, I focus on the ground beneath my feet. When I get to the edge between the gravel and the grass, I glance up. Kyle and Trey are sitting on the stone bench next to a weed-free flower bed. Chester sits like a statue in the middle of evenly spaced spikes of green stems.

"You finished it!"

Kyle crosses his arms over his chest and gives me a super-self-satisfied smile. "Yep. Dumped the weeds on the compost pile, put the tools away, and watered the flowers."

"All that's left to do is paint the fence." Trey wears the same proud smile.

"It looks good." I take a step forward and reach my hand up to high-five the garden crew. And topple over.

"Brandon!" Mom grabs for me as I face-plant in the grass. "I guess there's a learning curve with the cast, huh? Let's get you inside."

Taking up the entire couch, I rest my foot on a stack of pillows and stare at the blank TV screen. *Come to think of it, I've never seen the TV turned on.* I balance a glass of ice water on my stomach. The bendy straw might keep me from taking an ice water bath, but after the stunt on the lawn, I'm not feeling like the king of coordination.

The rest of the crew trickles in with drinks in their hands. Mom has her trademark cup of hot tea. Everyone else has something with ice in it. Mom scoots a chair closer to the couch so she's right beside me.

"You've had a busy couple of days, boys. Bekki and I searched for the secret passageways for years. You found them in a day."

"Yeah, but we had a secret weapon." I pat the couch and Chester hops up beside me.

"True. We didn't have the black and white wonder cat." Mom takes a sip of her tea "But, Brandon, you opened the puzzle box and figured out the clues on the map. And you're the one who figured out that the bad guys were after the pottery. How did you piece that together?"

"I don't know," I answer with a shrug. "It just came to me."

"What about the uncle? And his driver?" Mom frowns. "I remember meeting them the day we arrived."

"Both in jail." Aunt Sarah says. "I've been told they won't be getting out any time soon."

"So, they were after the pottery?"

Aunt Sarah nods. "Brandon was right. Miguel hid the emeralds in the pottery. His uncle gave the emeralds to Miguel to hold because he knew he was being watched by the Colombian police. Instead of giving them back to his uncle, Miguel sent them to America with me."

"When his uncle found out what he had done, he came to Colorado to try to steal them back. Somehow, he met the foreman at the Jones' vineyard, who was already using Smuggler's Gulch for some illegal activities. When the uncle heard the legends of secret passageways, he wanted this house." Aunt Sarah swirls the ice cubes in her water and then takes a long drink.

"He tried to strong arm me into selling the orchard and the house. When I turned him down, he decided he'd at least take what he came for. And try to scare me off the property."

"But his guy took the wrong one." Kyle turns the pottery jug in his hand. "This one is just a regular pitcher."

Lifting onto my elbows, I add, "And Aunt Sarah doesn't get scared."

Mom looks at me over her mug of tea. "Neither do you, I understand."

A warm flush spreads over me. "Not anymore." *God has not given us a spirit of fear, but of power, love and a sound mind.*

Alex has been quiet during the whole conversation, but when he pipes up, he asks what I'm aching to know. "Do you get to keep the coins and the emeralds, Aunt Sarah?"

"I do." Aunt Sarah's eyes mist with tears. "The coins are mine. And the initial valuation puts them at over ten thousand dollars. Maybe more." She sniffs and swipes at her eyes. "And the emeralds? Because of the work Joe and I did in Colombia, the Ambassador arranged a waiver of any legal claim to the gems. I'm waiting for an official appraisal, but they're worth a lot." She blinks, and a tear trickles down her cheek. "Enough that I can fix up the guest houses and renovate this old place."

"What are your plans for the house?" The look on Mom's face tells me she already has an idea.

"This old house is too big for one old lady to rattle around in by herself. And much too quiet. It needs children." Aunt Sarah winks at me and takes another sip of water. "Maybe I'll open an orphanage."

THE END

About the Author

Templa lives in Grand Junction, Colorado with her husband, Chris, their Miniature Australian Shepherd, Maggie, and a flock of extremely pampered chickens. She and her husband are Mimi and Granddad to five adorable and talented grandchildren. In addition to writing, Templa is an amateur artist who loves to paint while singing off-key to worship music.

Templa is a member of Word Weavers International and American Christian Fiction Writers. Her first novel, *Season of Forgiveness*, was published in 2014. *The Orchard's Secret* is her first mystery novella. You can find her at www.TemplaMelnick.com.

LOOK FOR THESE GREAT BOOKS FROM BROKEN YOKE PUBLISHING.

Rocky Mountain Medley Novella Collection

Uranium Downs *by Jessica Bertrand*
Interruption *by Robin Densmore Fuson*
The Orchard's Secret *by Templa Melnick*
Price of Grace *by Debra Shelton*

Books by Templa Melnick

Seasons in Riverbend Series
   Season of Forgiveness
   Season of Redemption *(coming soon)*

Ezekiel's Valley Series
   Ezekiel's Valley *(coming soon)*

Books by Chris Melnick

The Messianic Passover Celebration – Leader's Manual
The Messianic Passover Celebration – Participant Handbook

BROKEN YOKE

PUBLISHING

brokenyokepublishing.com

www.ingramcontent.com/pod-product-compliance
Lightning Source LLC
Chambersburg PA
CBHW021035130626
46552CB00005B/1862